BANANA FOX AND THE SECRET SOUR SOCIETY

JAMES KOCHALKA

graphix

An Imprint of

SCHOLASTIC

For Nooko, Hermie, and Wendy

Library of Congress Control Number: 2019957499

ISBN 978-1-338-66049-4 (hardcover)
ISBN 978-1-338-66048-7 (paperback)

10 9 8 7 6 5 4 3 2   21 22 23 24 25

Printed in China   62
First edition, January 2021

Edited by Megan Peace
Book design by Steve Ponzo
Creative Director: Phil Falco
Publisher: David Saylor

CONTENTS

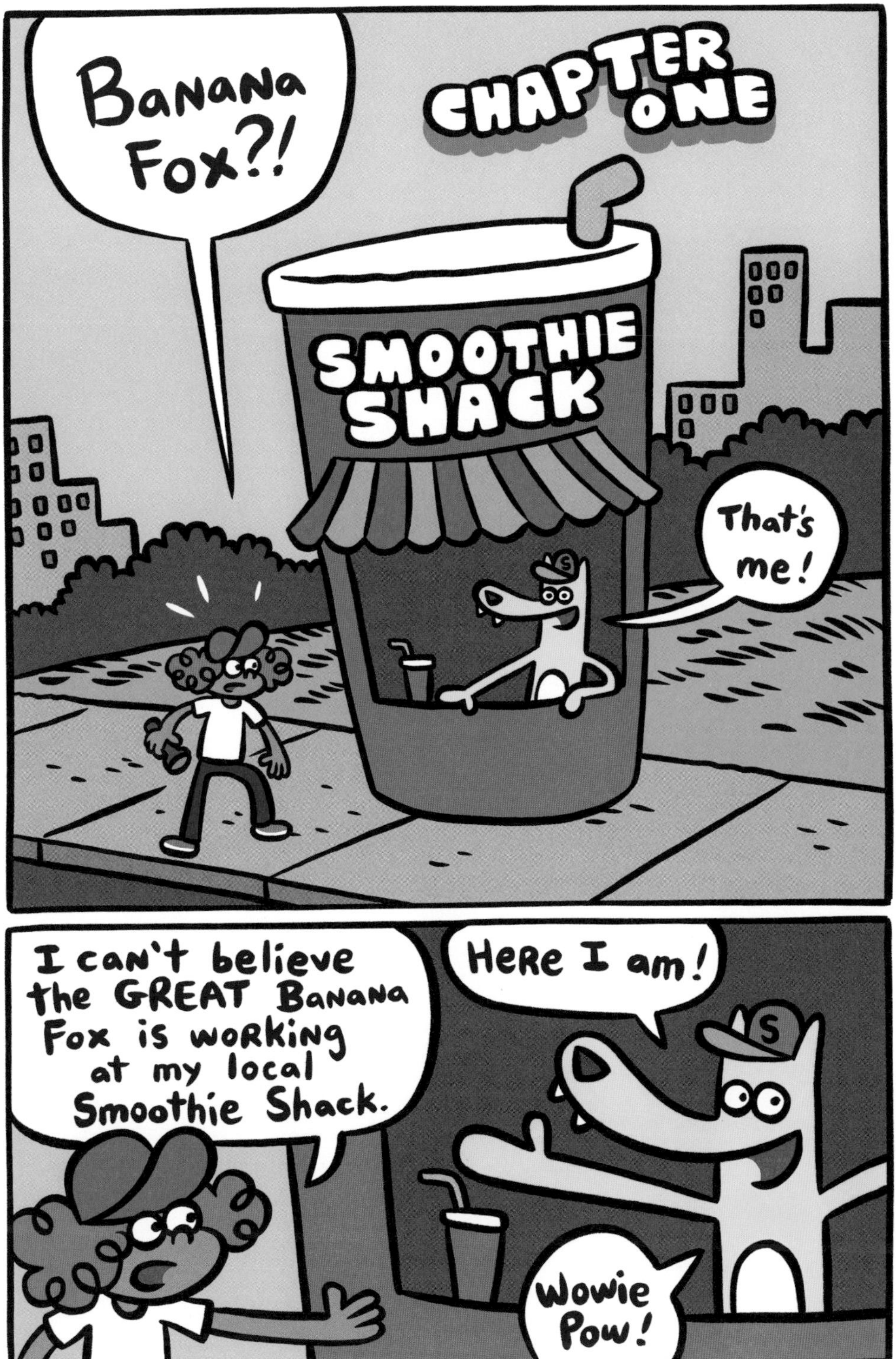
CHAPTER ONE
Banana Fox?!
SMOOTHIE SHACK
That's me!
I can't believe the GREAT Banana Fox is working at my local Smoothie Shack.
Here I am!
Wowie Pow!

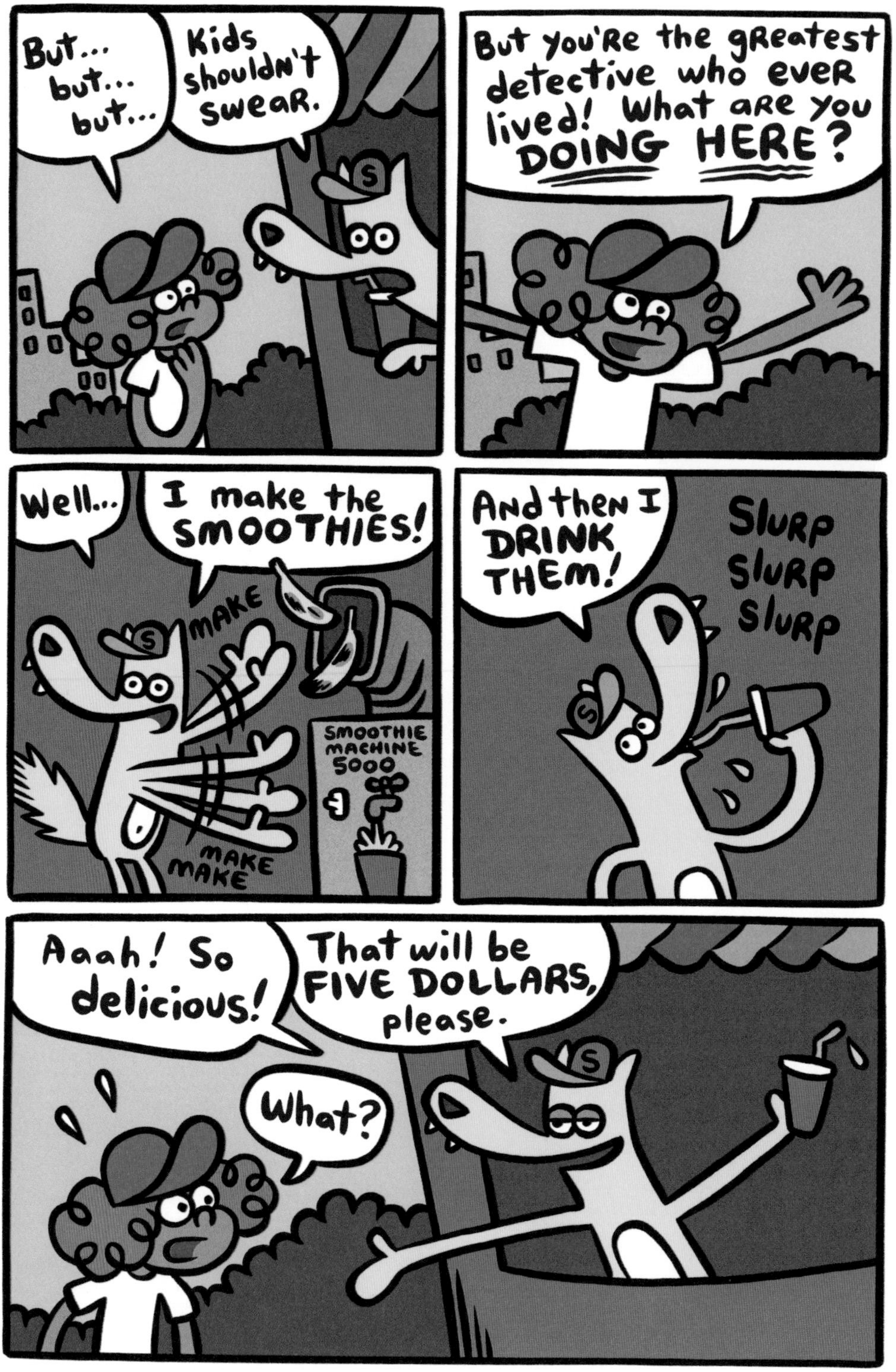
But... but... but...
Kids shouldn't swear.
But you're the greatest detective who ever lived! What are you DOING HERE?
Well...
I make the SMOOTHIES!
MAKE
MAKE MAKE
SMOOTHIE MACHINE 5000
And then I DRINK THEM!
Slurp slurp slurp
Aaah! So delicious!
That will be FIVE DOLLARS, please.
What?

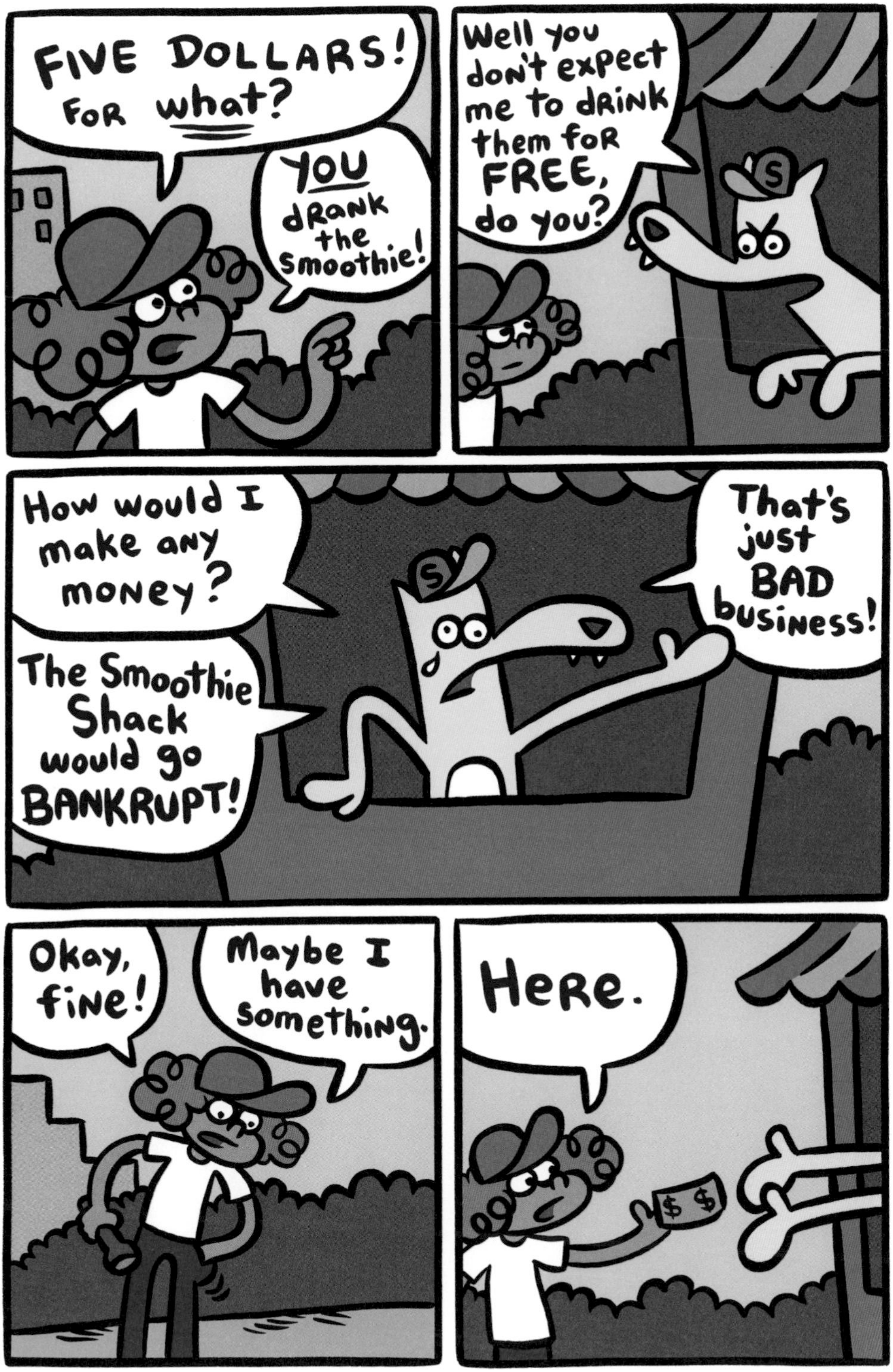
FIVE DOLLARS! For what?
YOU drank the smoothie!
Well you don't expect me to drink them for FREE, do you?
How would I make any money?
The Smoothie Shack would go BANKRUPT!
That's just BAD business!
Okay, fine!
Maybe I have something.
Here.
S
$ $

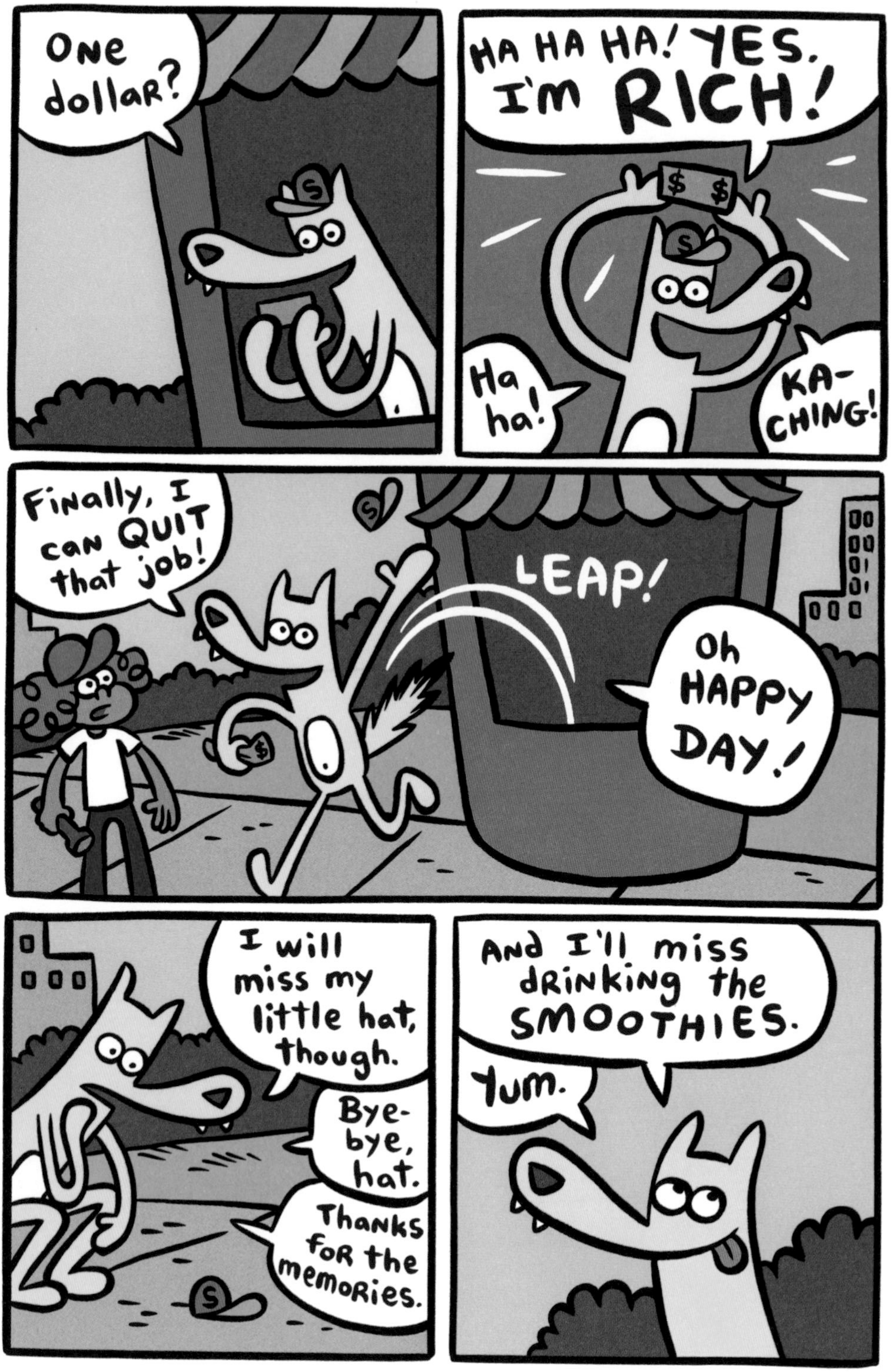
One dollar?
HA HA HA! YES, I'M RICH!
Ha ha!
KA-CHING!
Finally, I can QUIT that job!
LEAP!
Oh HAPPY DAY!
I will miss my little hat, though.
Bye-bye, hat.
Thanks for the memories.
And I'll miss drinking the SMOOTHIES.
Yum.

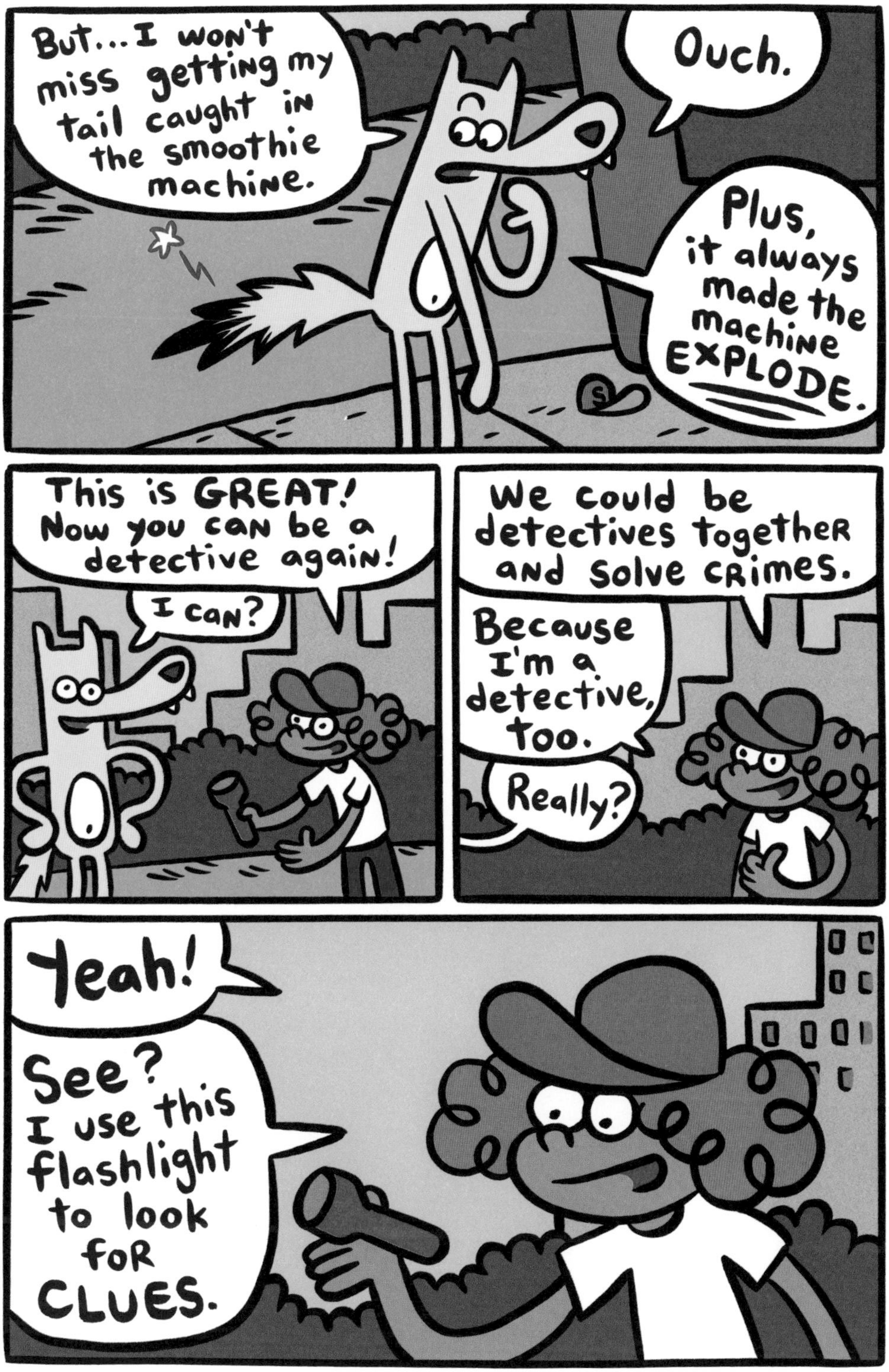
But...I won't miss getting my tail caught in the smoothie machine.
Ouch.
Plus, it always made the machine EXPLODE.
S
This is GREAT! Now you can be a detective again!
I can?
We could be detectives together and solve crimes.
Because I'm a detective, too.
Really?
Yeah!
See? I use this flashlight to look for CLUES.

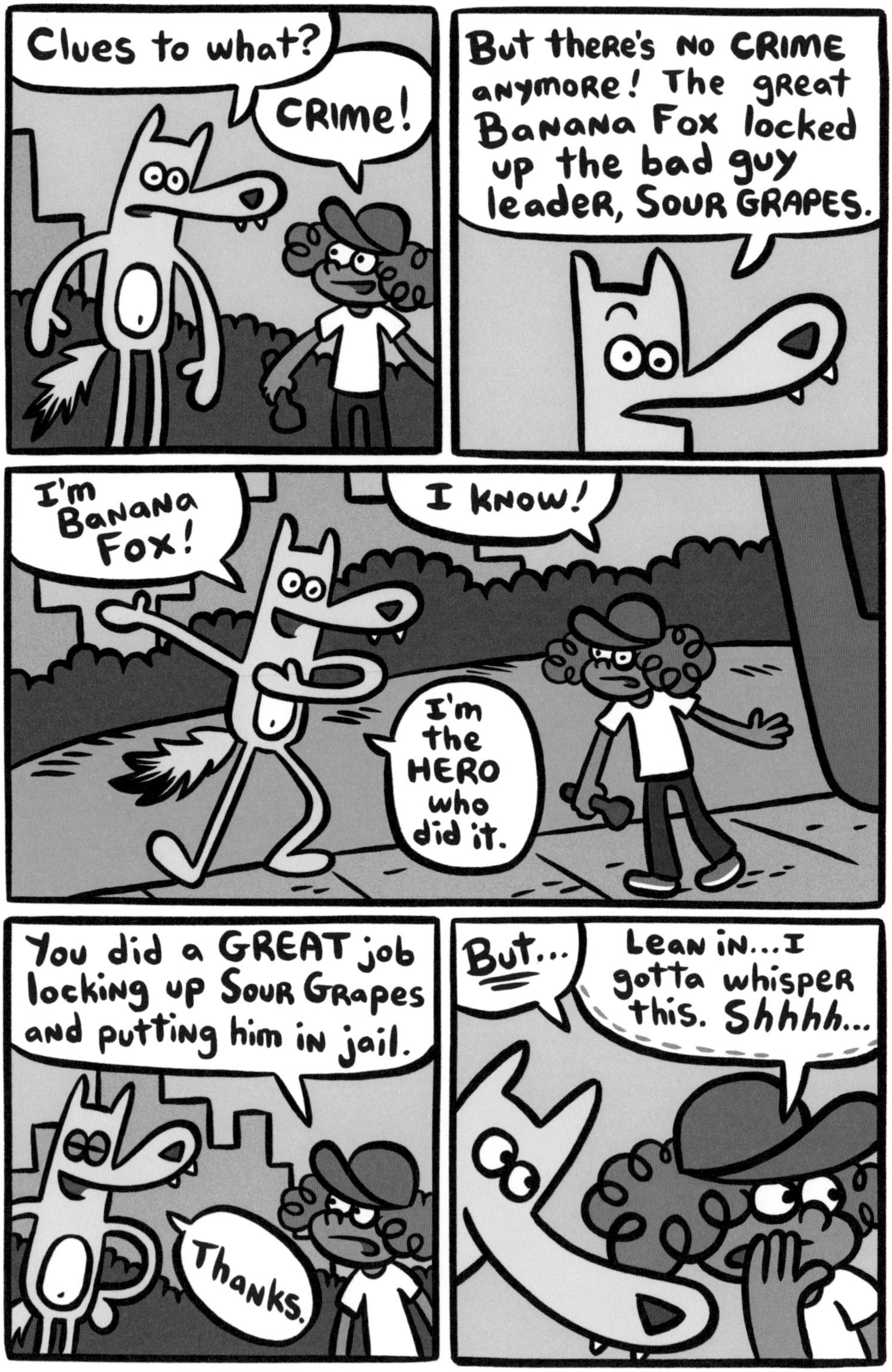
Clues to what?
CRIME!
But there's NO CRIME anymore! The great Banana Fox locked up the bad guy leader, SOUR GRAPES.
I'm Banana Fox!
I KNOW!
I'm the HERO who did it.
You did a GREAT job locking up Sour Grapes and putting him in jail.
Thanks.
But...
Lean in... I gotta whisper this. Shhhh...

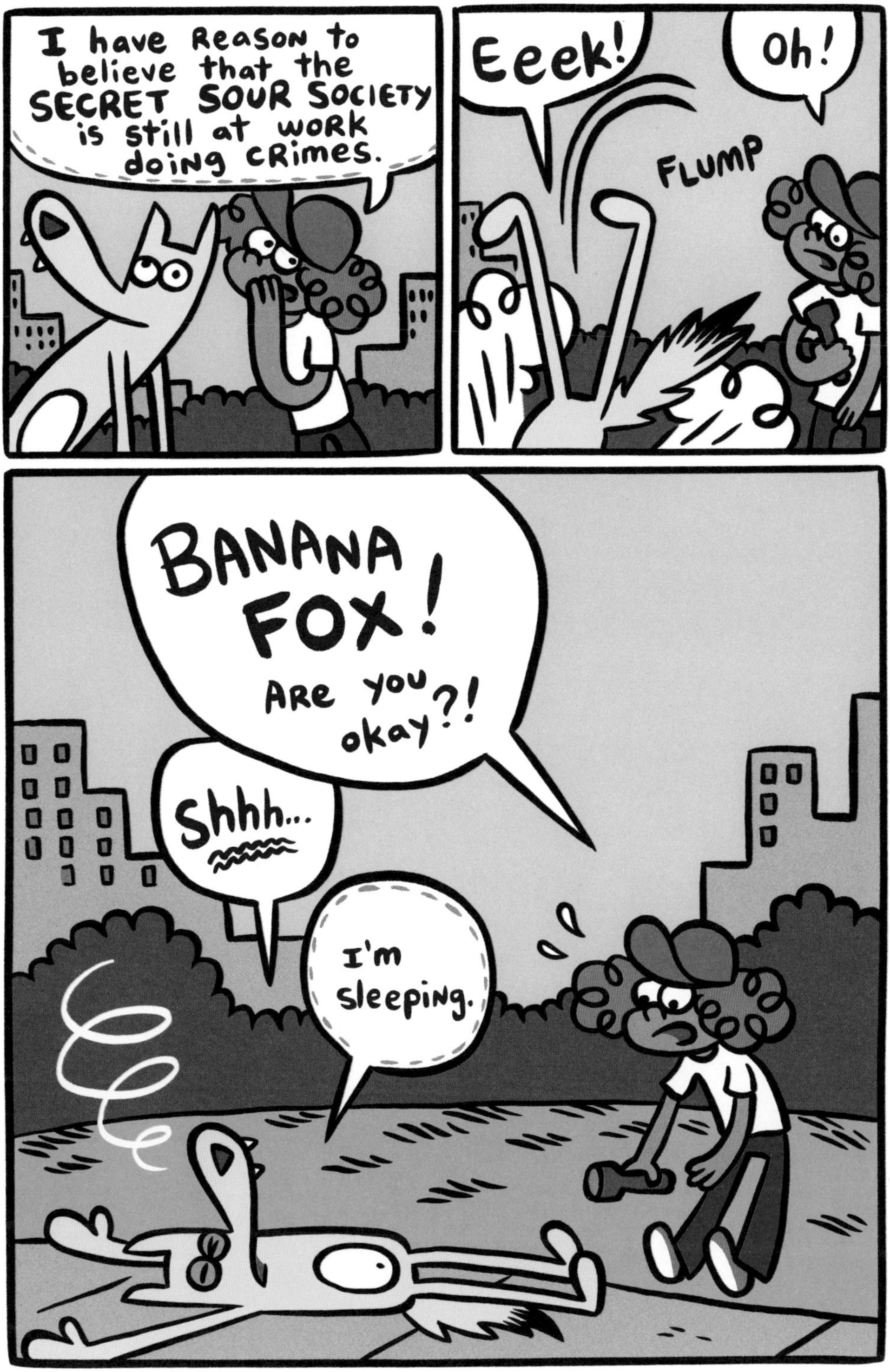
I have Reason to believe that the SECRET SOUR SOCIETY is still at work doing crimes.
Eeek!
Oh!
FLUMP
BANANA FOX! Are you okay?!
Shhh...
I'm sleeping.

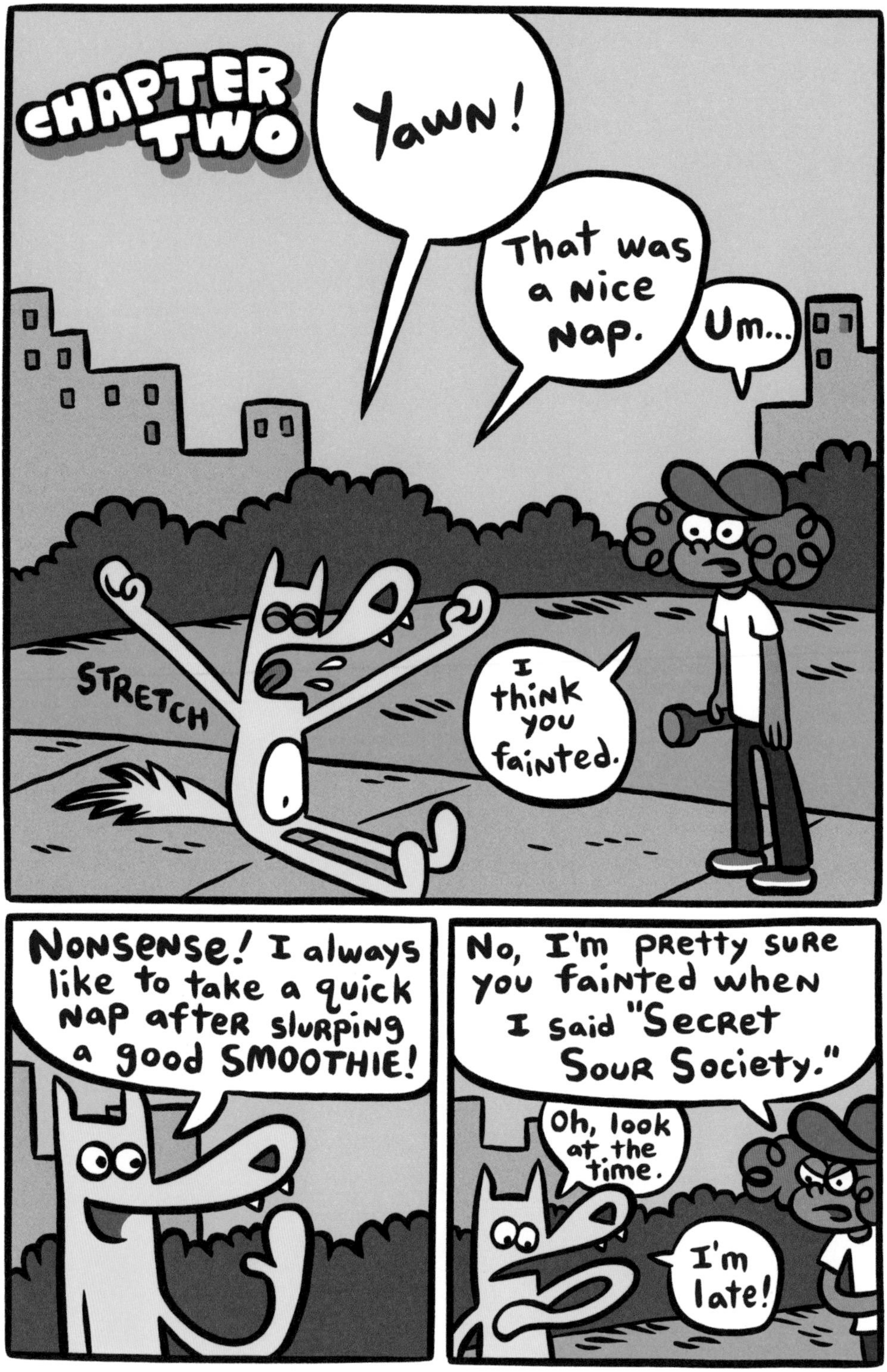
CHAPTER TWO
Yawn!
That was a nice nap.
Um...
STRETCH
I think you fainted.
Nonsense! I always like to take a quick nap after slurping a good SMOOTHIE!
No, I'm pretty sure you fainted when I said "Secret Sour Society."
Oh, look at the time.
I'm late!

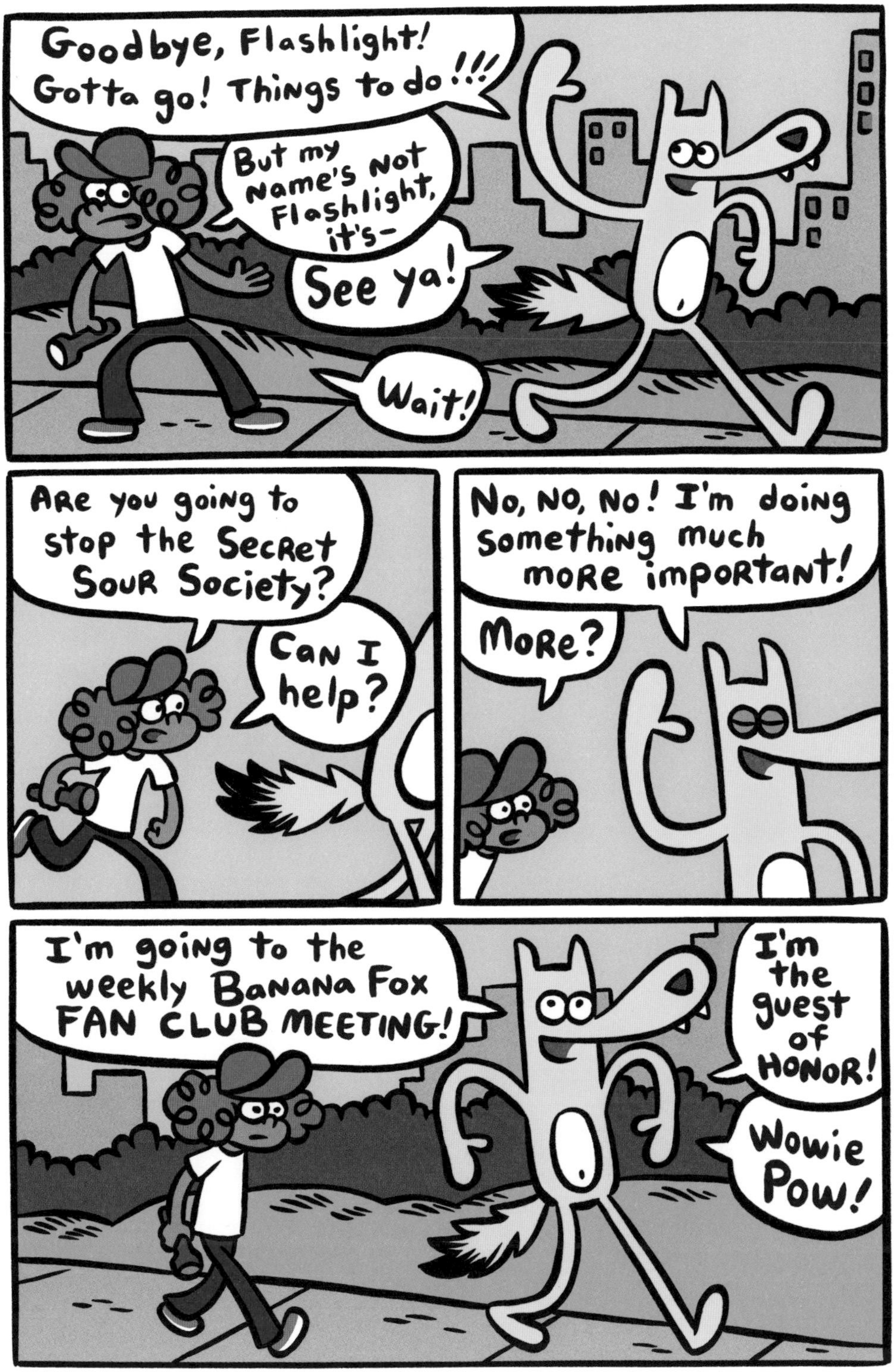
Goodbye, Flashlight! Gotta go! Things to do!!!
But my name's not Flashlight, it's-
See ya!
Wait!
Are you going to stop the Secret Sour Society?
Can I help?
No, NO, No! I'm doing something much more important!
More?
I'm going to the weekly Banana Fox FAN CLUB MEETING!
I'm the guest of HONOR!
Wowie Pow!

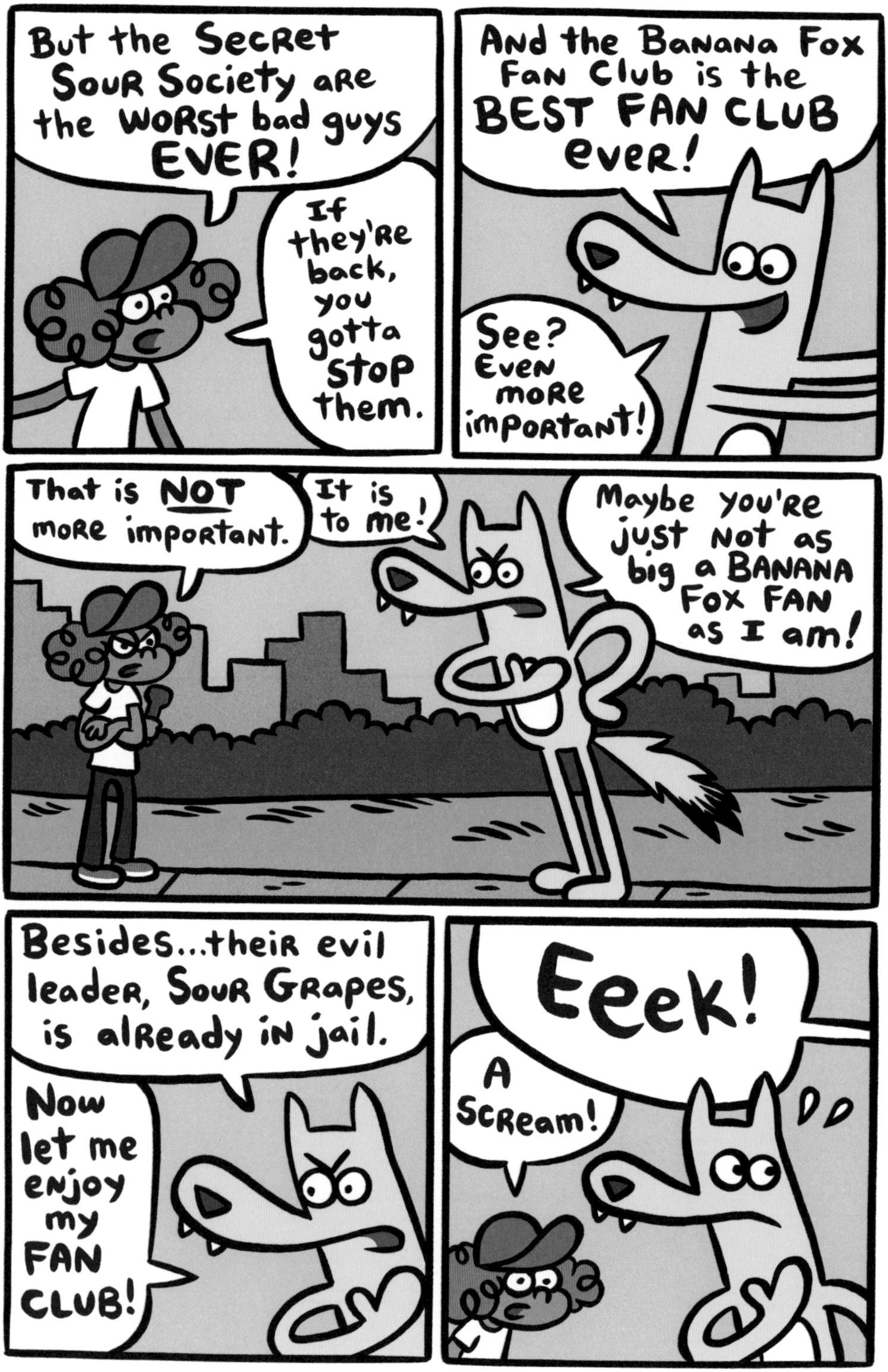
But the Secret Sour Society are the WORST bad guys EVER!
If they're back, you gotta STOP them.
And the Banana Fox Fan Club is the BEST FAN CLUB ever!
See? Even more important!
That is NOT more important.
It is to me!
Maybe you're just not as big a BANANA FOX FAN as I am!
Besides...their evil leader, Sour Grapes, is already in jail.
Now let me enjoy my FAN CLUB!
Eeek!
A Scream!

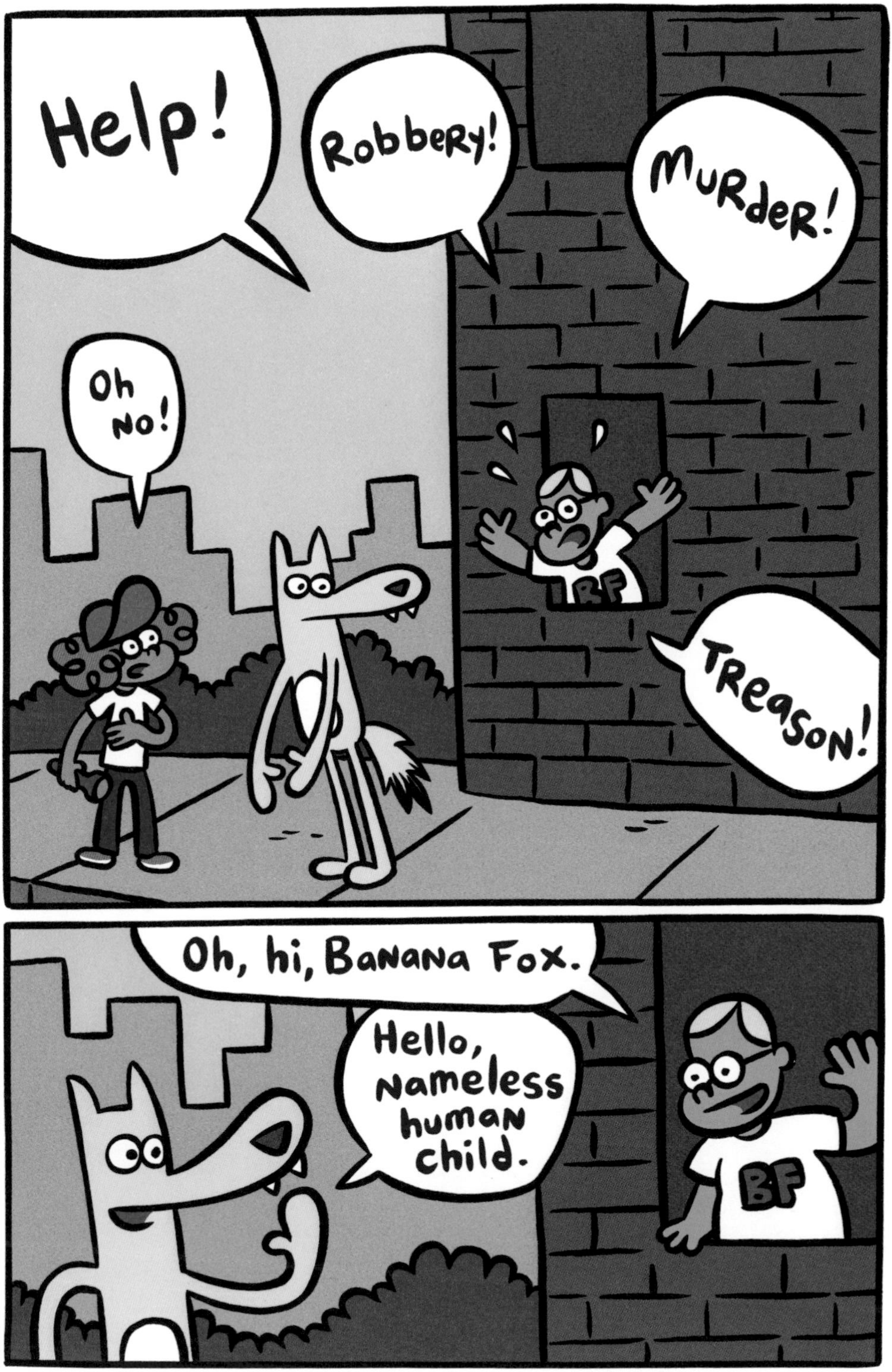
Help!
Robbery!
Murder!
Oh no!
Treason!
Oh, hi, Banana Fox.
Hello, nameless human child.
BF

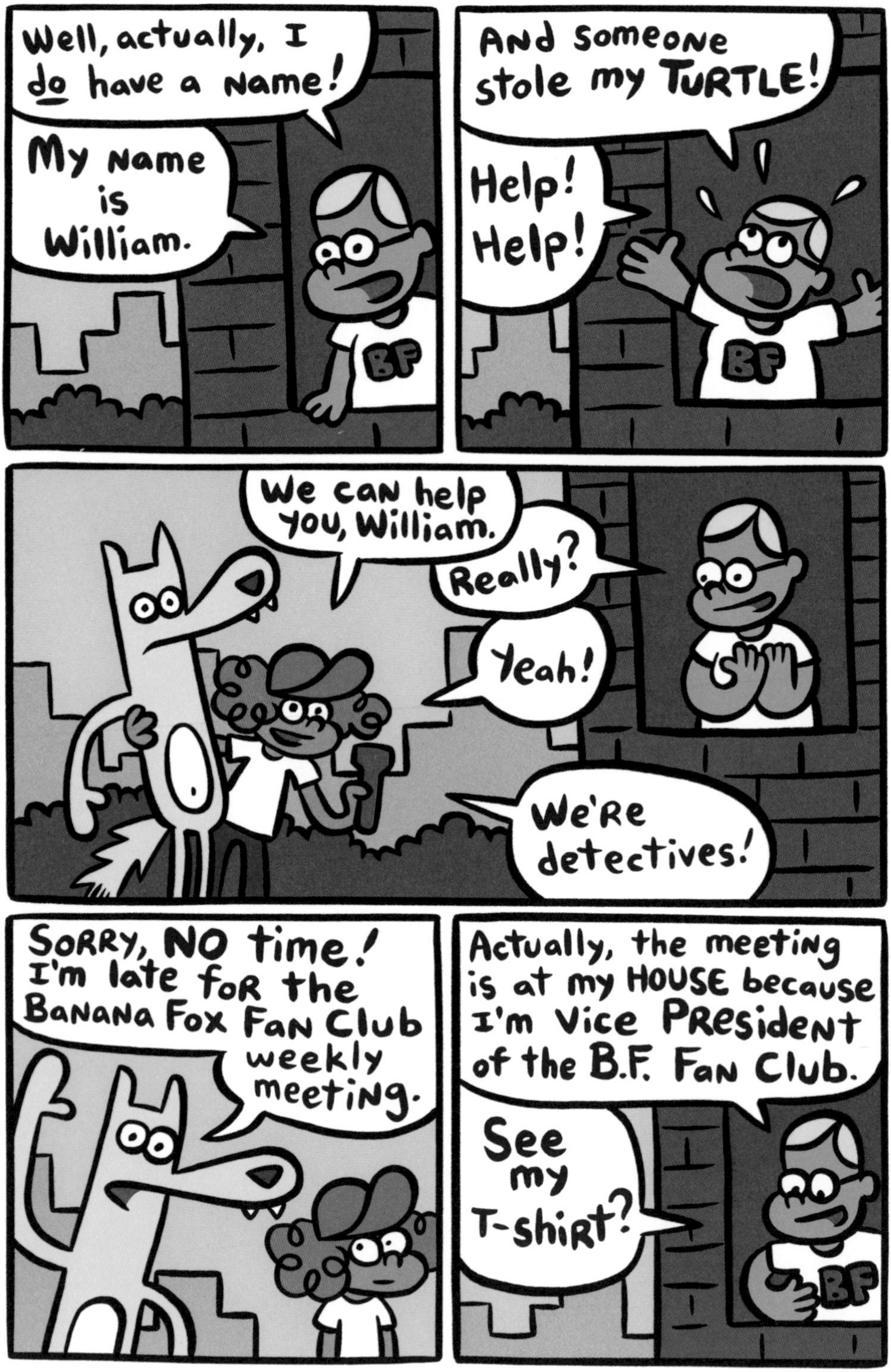
Well, actually, I do have a Name!
My Name is William.
And someone stole my TURTLE!
Help! Help!
We can help you, William.
Really?
Yeah!
We're detectives!
SORRY, NO time! I'm late for the Banana Fox Fan Club weekly meeting.
Actually, the meeting is at my HOUSE because I'm Vice PRESident of the B.F. Fan Club.
See my T-shirt?

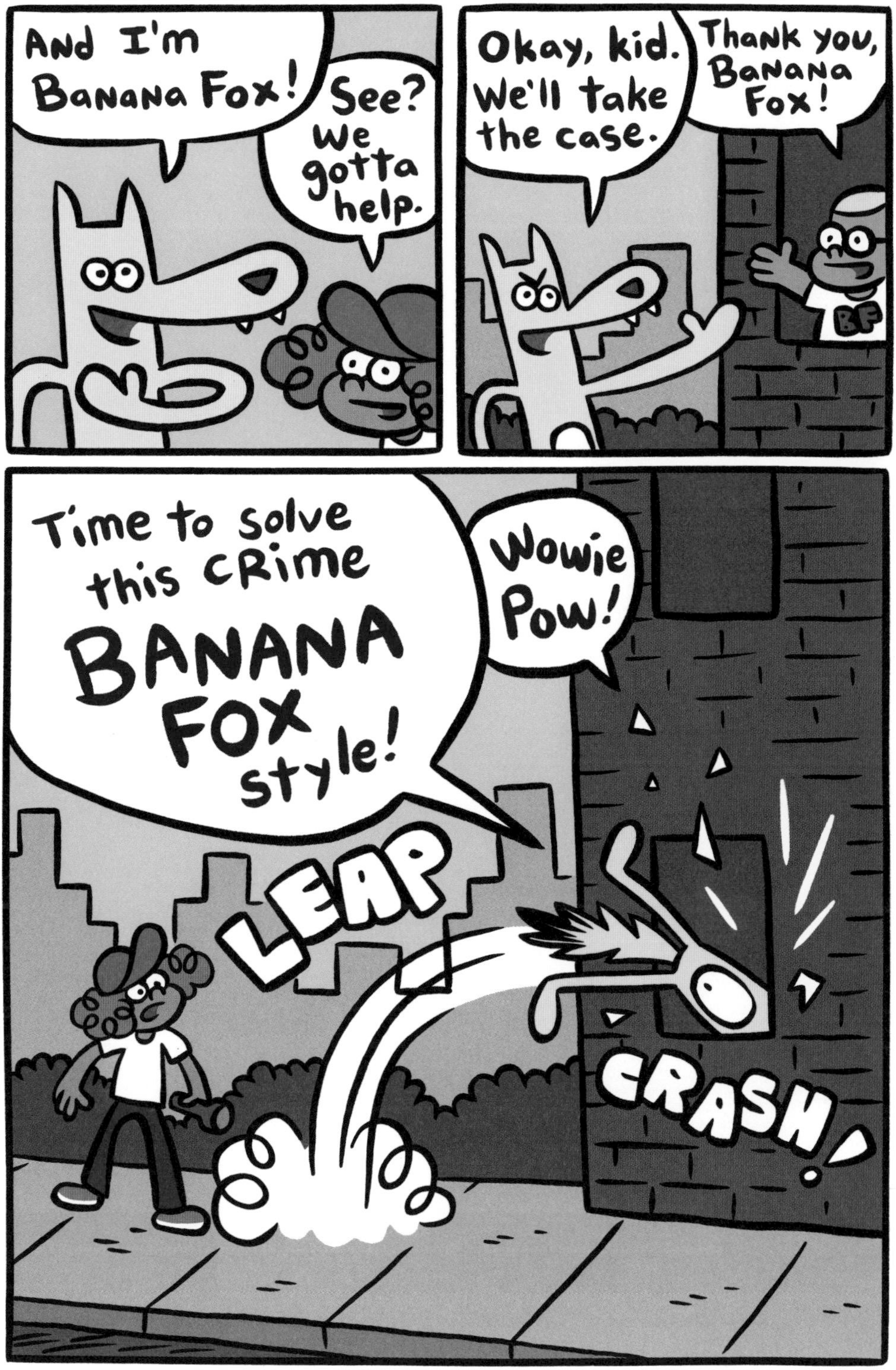
And I'm Banana Fox!
See? We gotta help.
Okay, kid. We'll take the case.
Thank you, Banana Fox!
Time to solve this crime BANANA FOX style!
Wowie Pow!
LEAP
CRASH!

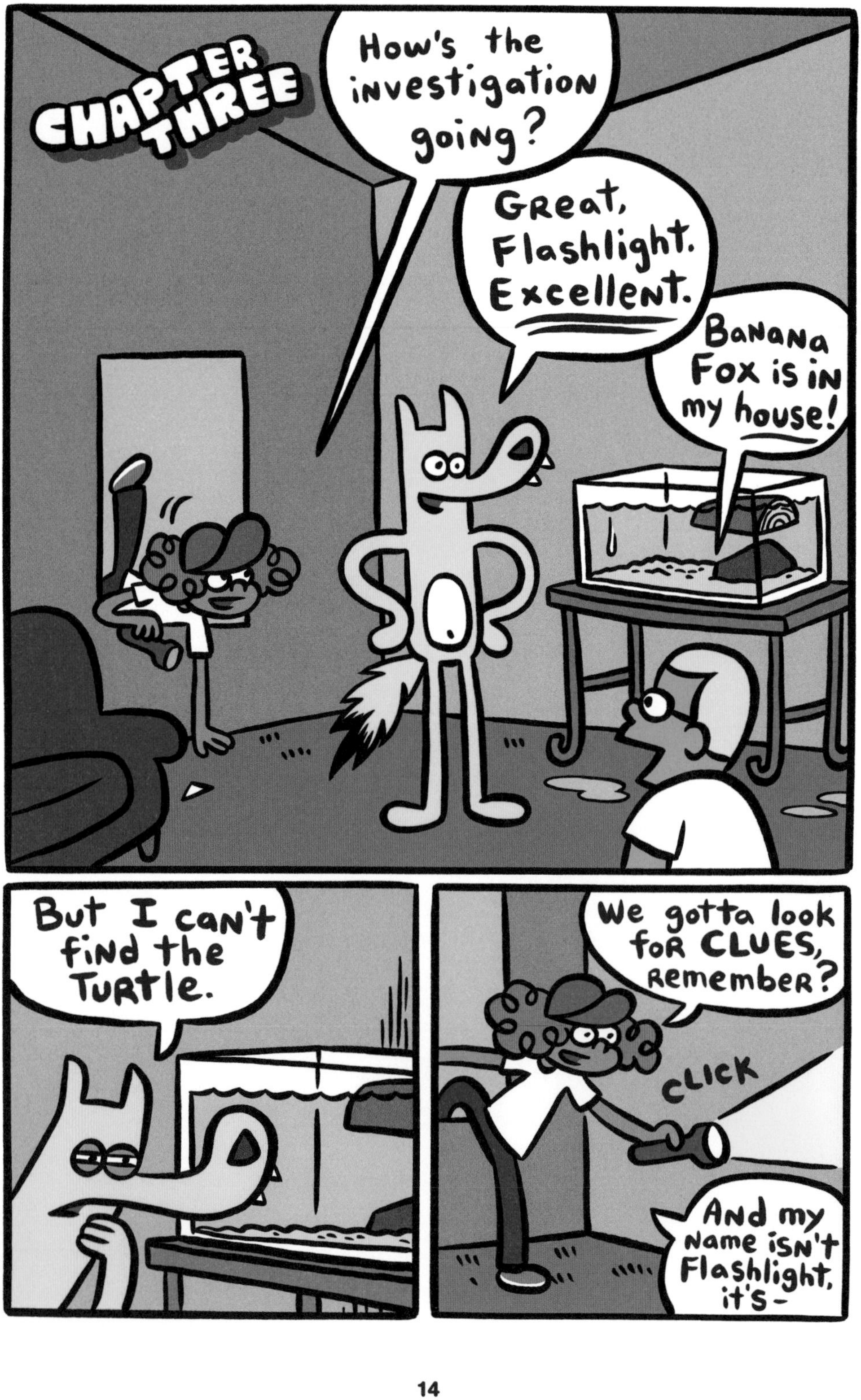
CHAPTER THREE
How's the investigation going?
Great, Flashlight. Excellent.
Banana Fox is in my house!
But I can't find the Turtle.
We gotta look for CLUES, remember?
CLICK
And my name isn't Flashlight, it's -

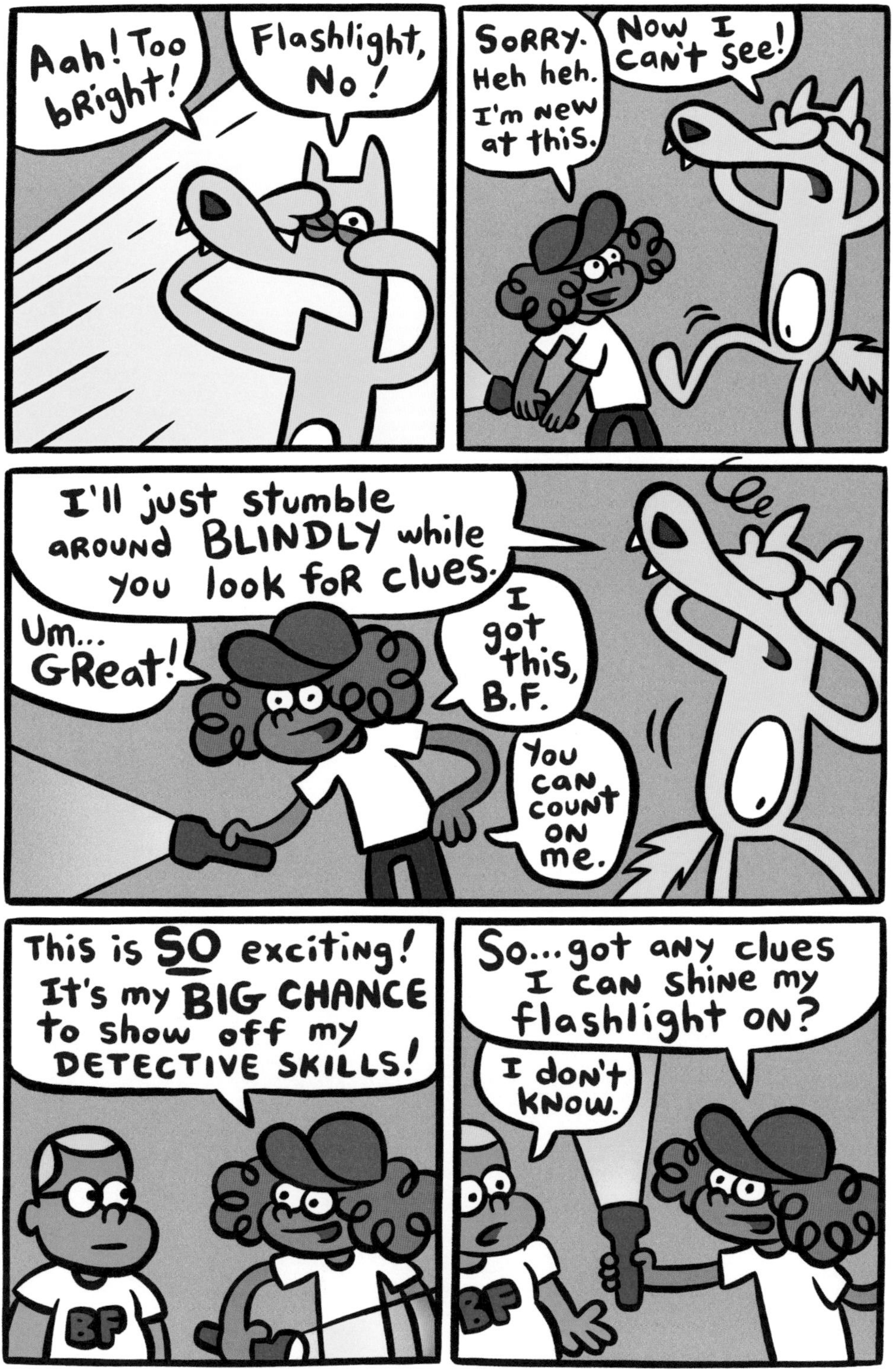
Aah! Too bRight!
Flashlight, No!
SoRRy. Heh heh. I'm new at this.
Now I can't see!
I'll just stumble around BLINDLY while you look foR clues.
Um... GReat!
I got this, B.F.
You can count on me.
This is SO exciting! It's my BIG CHANCE to show off my DETECTIVE SKILLS!
So...got any clues I can shine my flashlight on?
I don't know.
BF

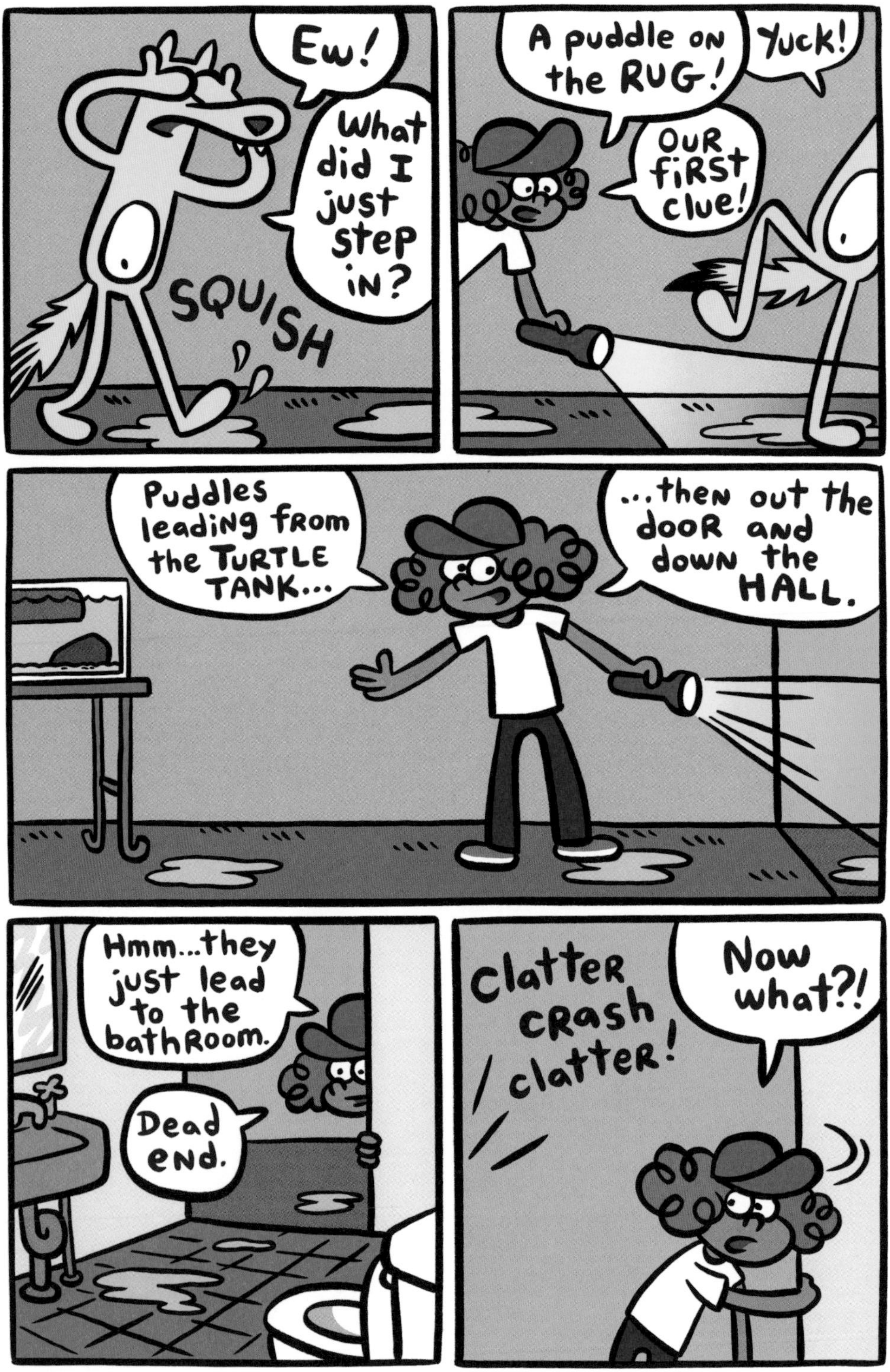
Ew!
What did I just step in?
SQUISH
A puddle on the RUG!
Yuck!
OUR FIRST clue!
Puddles leading from the TURTLE TANK...
...then out the door and down the HALL.
Hmm...they just lead to the bathroom.
Dead end.
Clatter crash clatter!
Now what?!

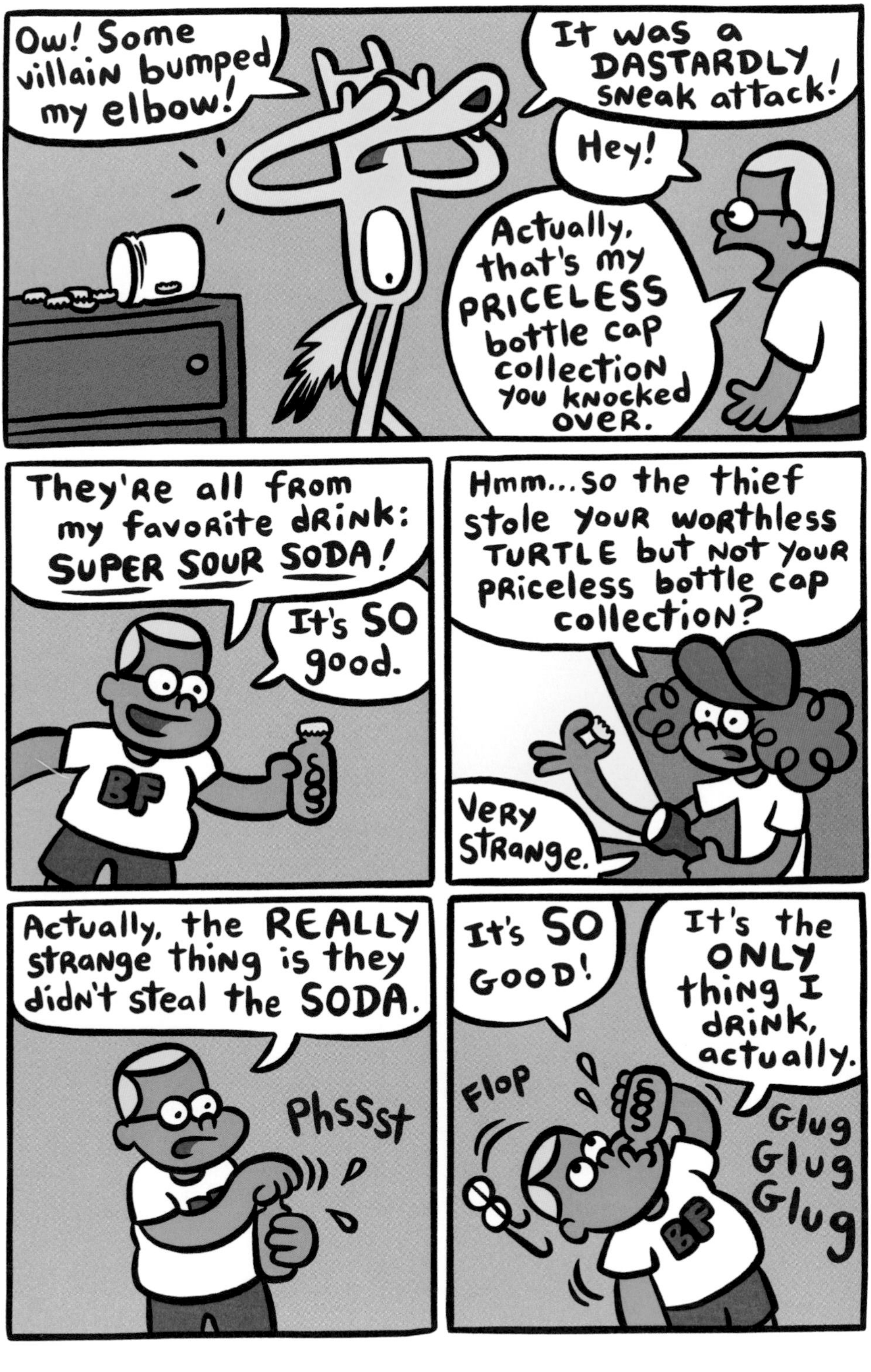
Ow! Some villain bumped my elbow!
It was a DASTARDLY sneak attack!
Hey!
Actually, that's my PRICELESS bottle cap collection you knocked over.
They're all from my favorite drink: SUPER SOUR SODA!
It's SO good.
Hmm...so the thief stole your worthless TURTLE but not your priceless bottle cap collection?
Very strange.
Actually, the REALLY strange thing is they didn't steal the SODA.
Phssst
It's SO GOOD!
It's the ONLY thing I drink, actually.
Flop
Glug
Glug
Glug

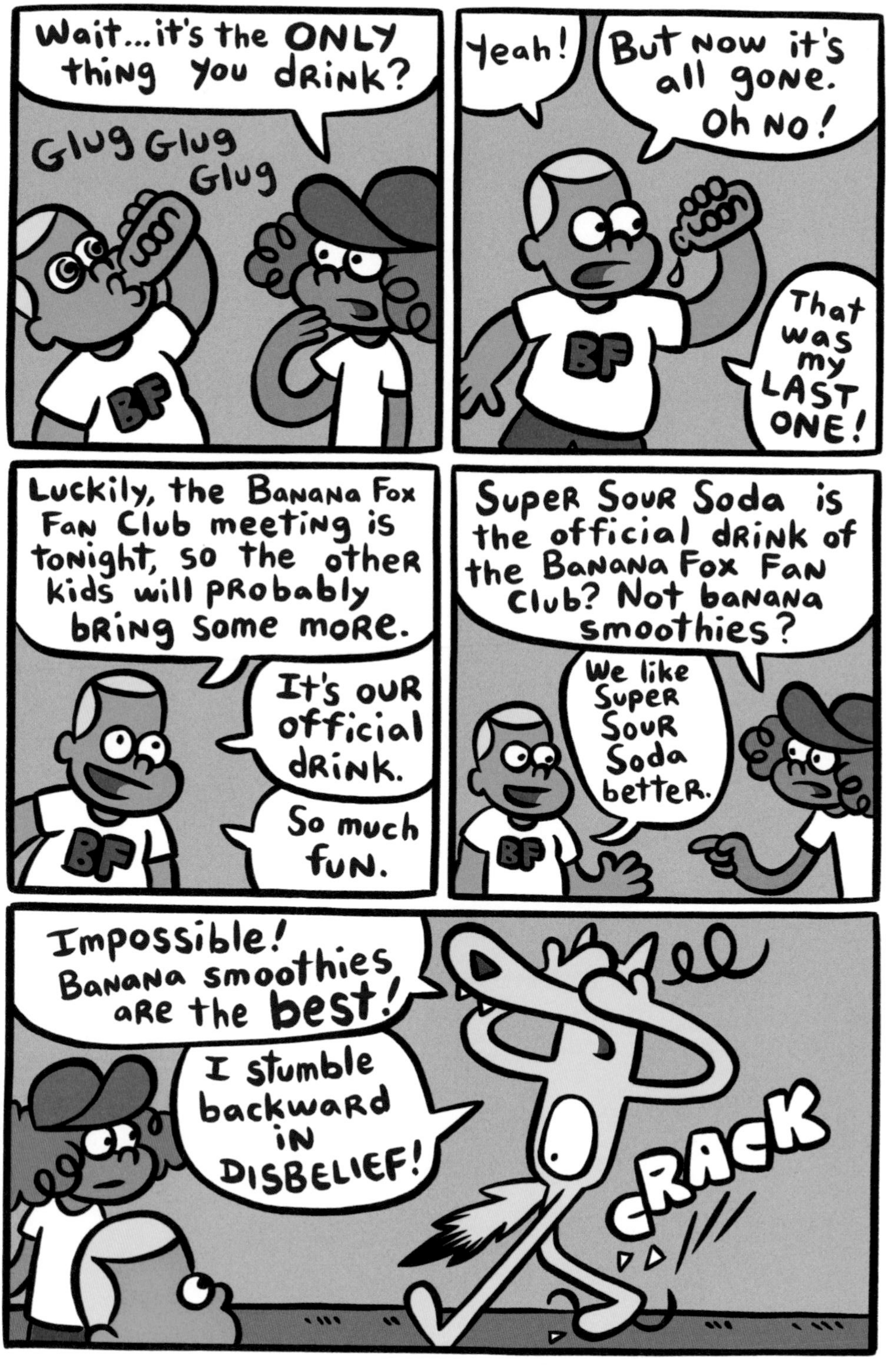

Wait... it's the ONLY thing you drink?
Glug Glug Glug
Yeah!
But now it's all gone. Oh no!
That was my LAST ONE!
Luckily, the Banana Fox Fan Club meeting is tonight, so the other kids will probably bring some more.
It's our official drink.
So much fun.
Super Sour Soda is the official drink of the Banana Fox Fan Club? Not banana smoothies?
We like Super Sour Soda better.
BF
Impossible! Banana smoothies are the best!
I stumble backward in DISBELIEF!
CRACK

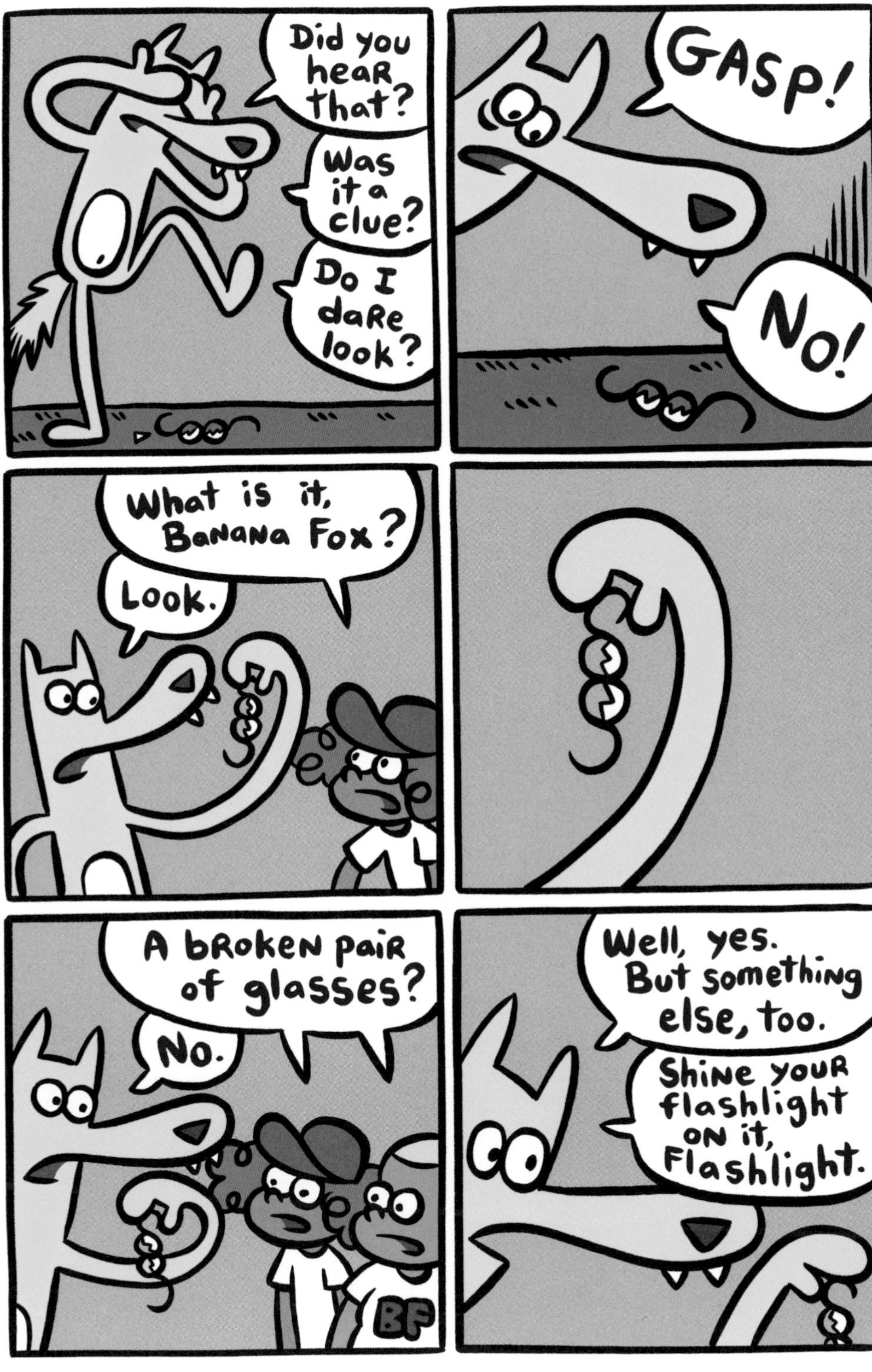
Did you hear that?
Was it a clue?
Do I dare look?
GASP!
No!
What is it, Banana Fox?
Look.
A broken pair of glasses?
No.
Well, yes. But something else, too.
Shine your flashlight on it, Flashlight.
BF

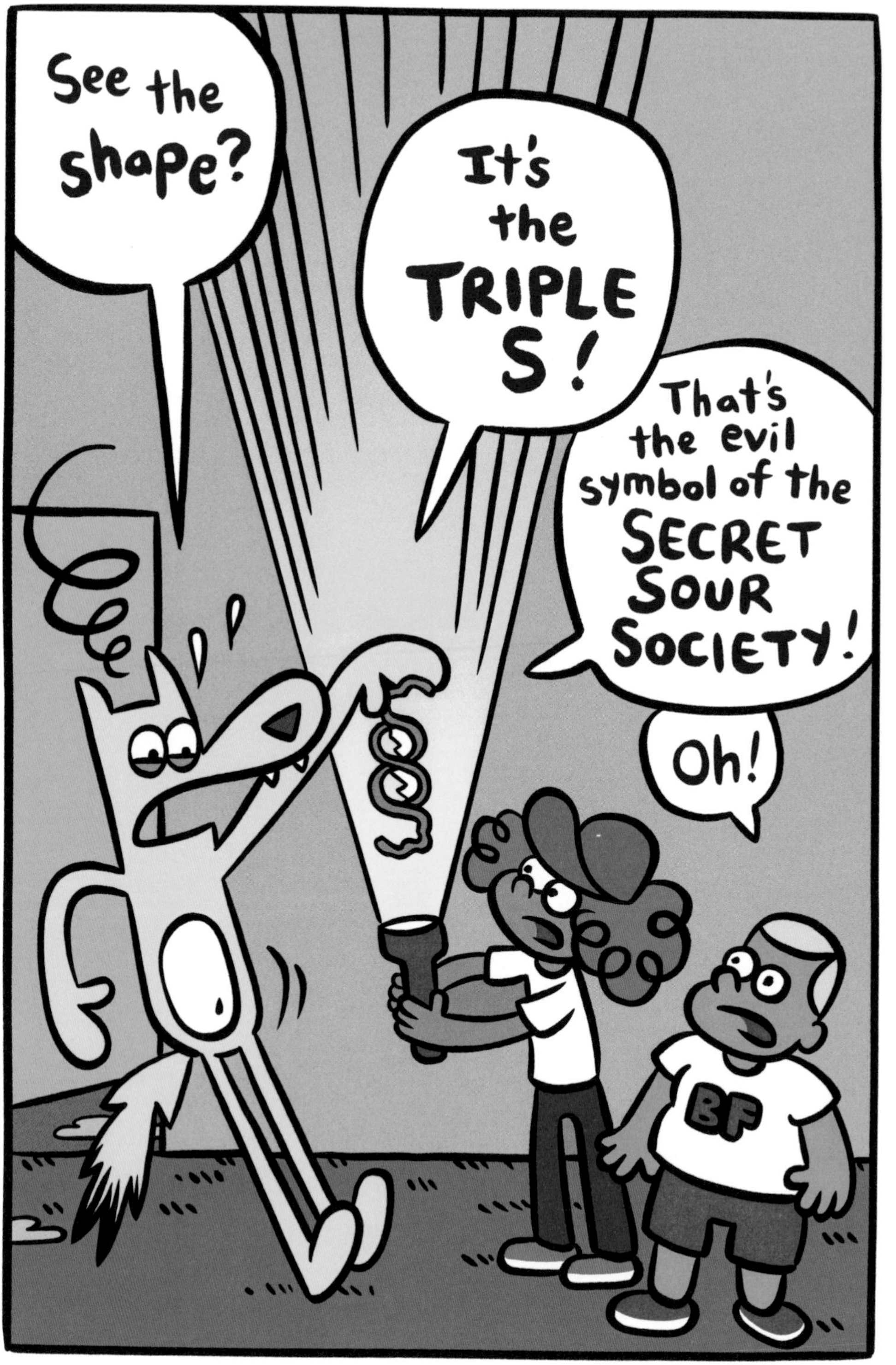
See the shape?
It's the TRIPLE S!
That's the evil symbol of the SECRET SOUR SOCIETY!
Oh!
BF

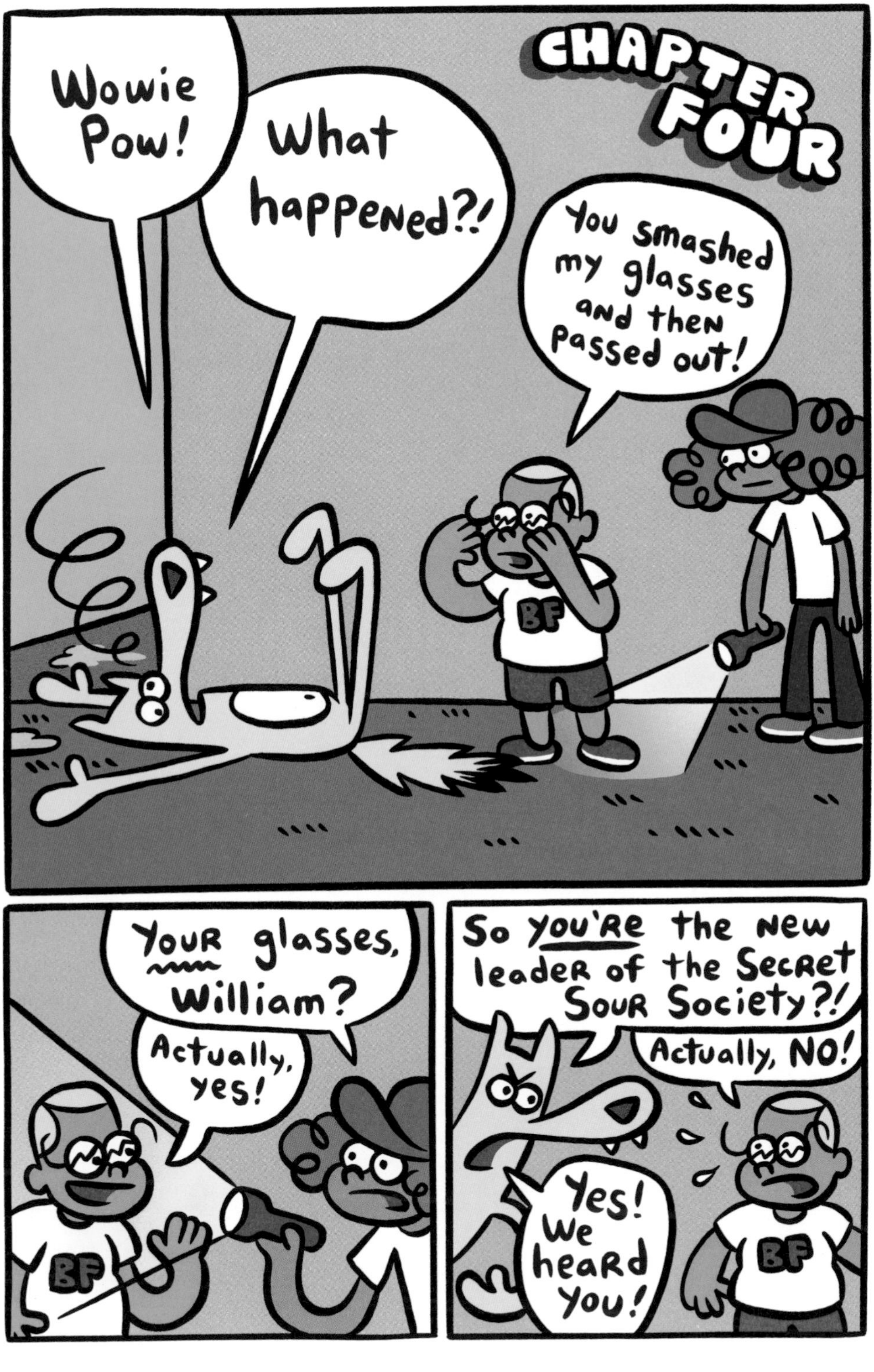
CHAPTER FOUR
Wowie Pow!
What happened?!
You smashed my glasses and then passed out!
YOUR glasses, William?
Actually, yes!
So YOU'RE the new leader of the Secret Sour Society?!
Actually, NO!
Yes! We heard you!

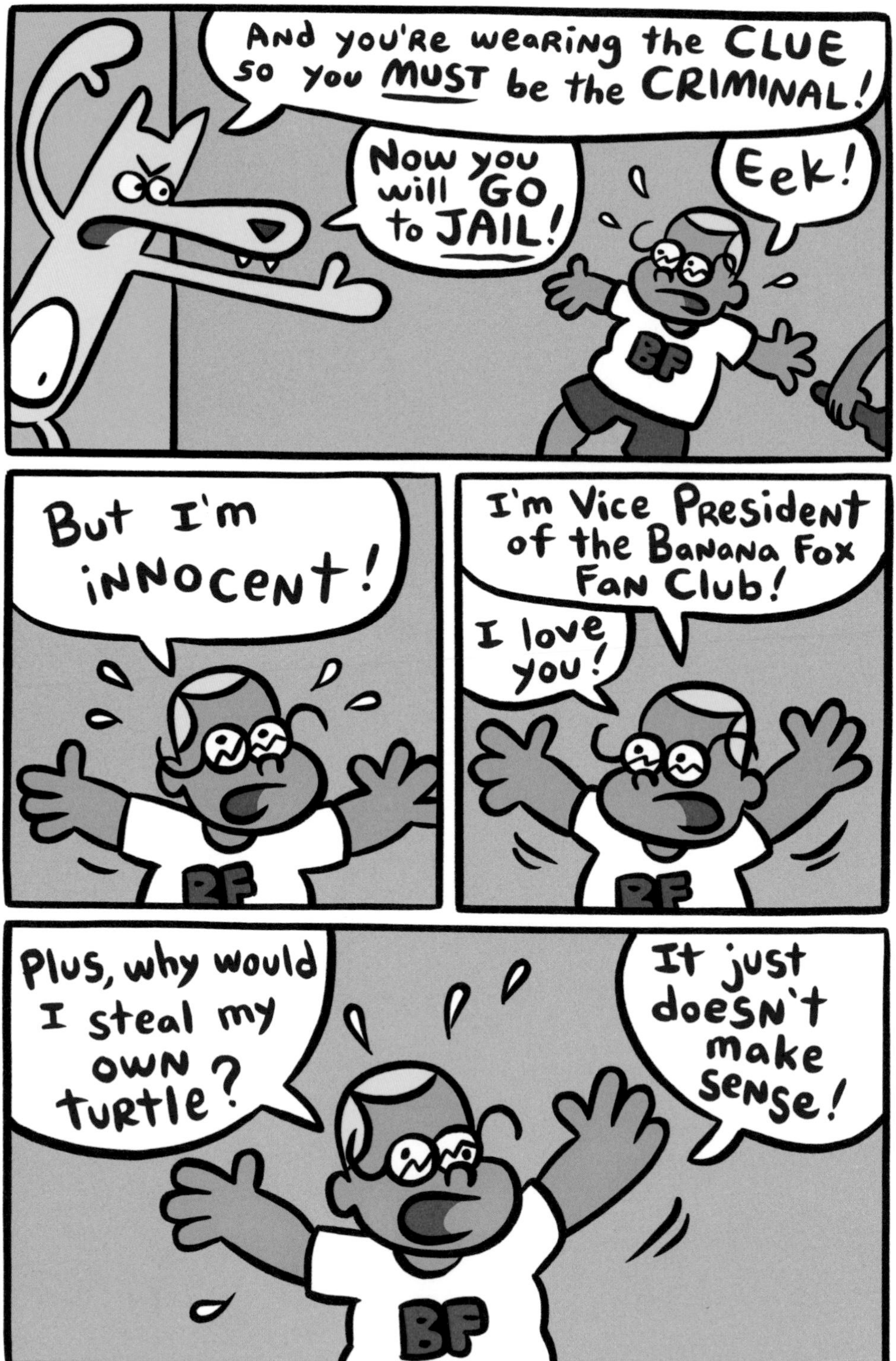
And you're wearing the CLUE so you MUST be the CRIMINAL!
Now you will GO to JAIL!
Eek!
But I'm innocent!
I'm Vice President of the Banana Fox Fan Club!
I love you!
Plus, why would I steal my own turtle?
It just doesn't make sense!

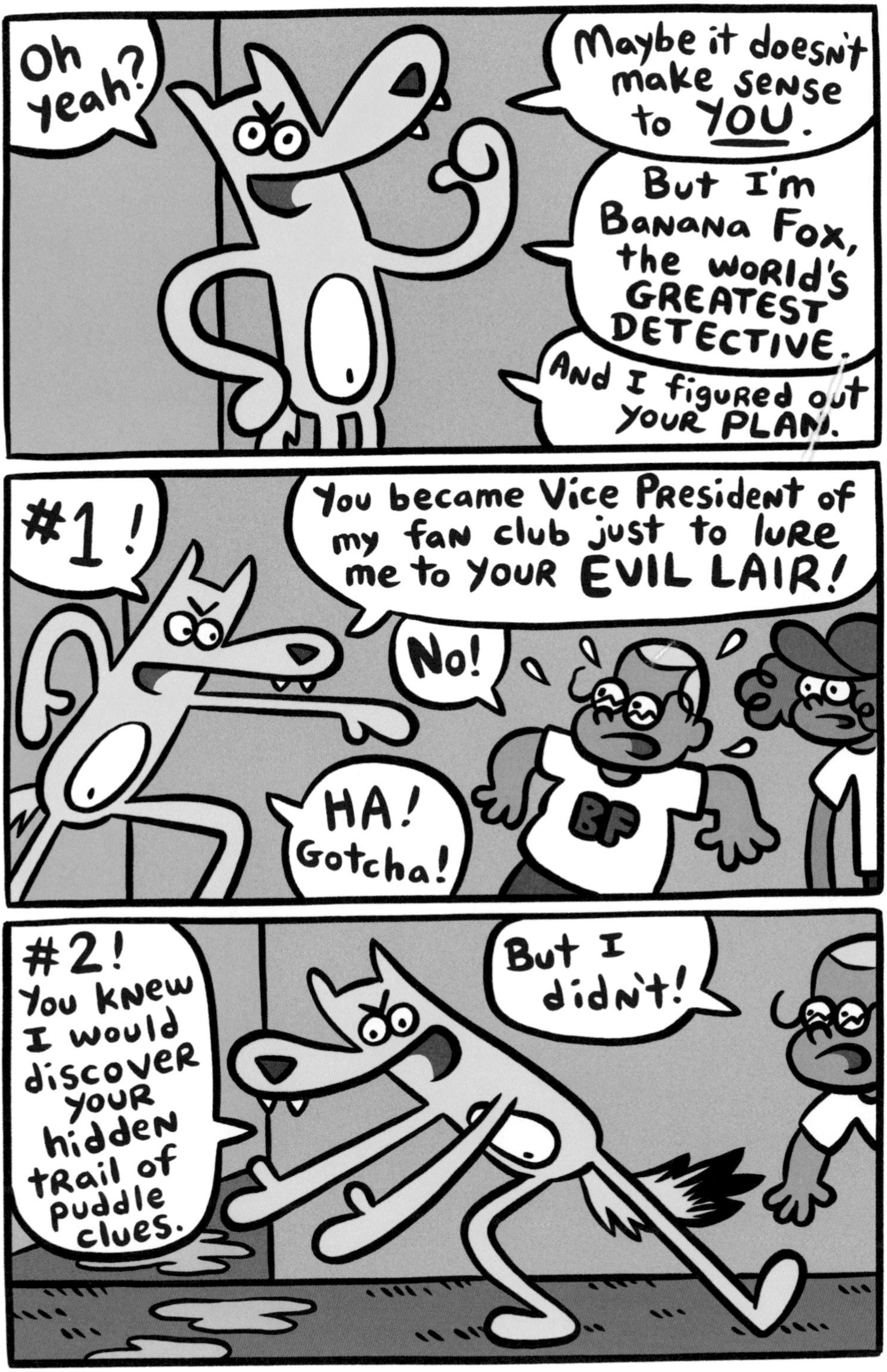
Oh yeah?
Maybe it doesn't make sense to YOU.
But I'm Banana Fox, the world's GREATEST DETECTIVE.
And I figured out your PLAN.
#1!
You became Vice President of my fan club just to lure me to your EVIL LAIR!
No!
HA! Gotcha!
BF
#2! You knew I would discover your hidden trail of puddle clues.
But I didn't!

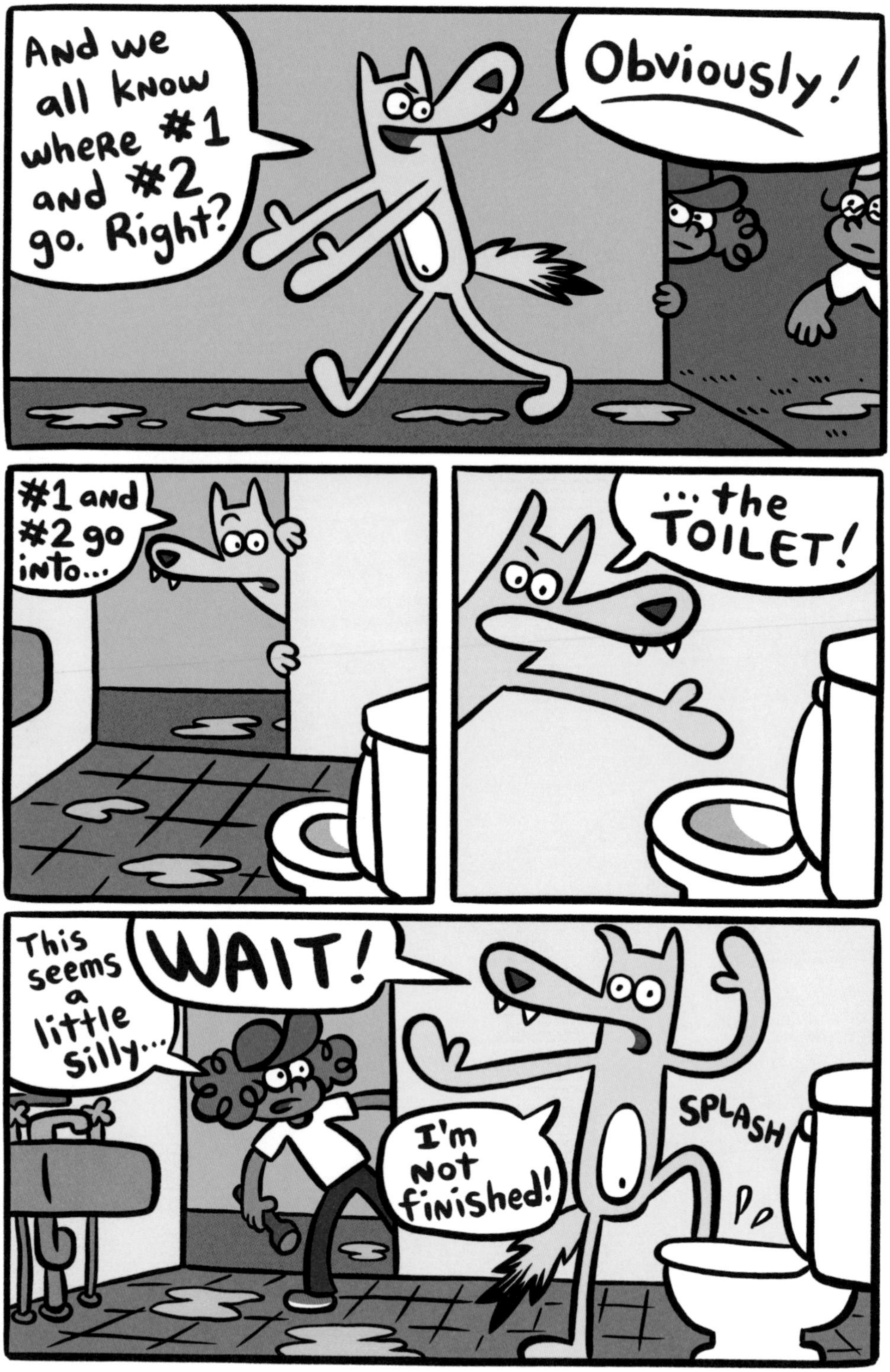
And we all know where #1 and #2 go. Right?
Obviously!
#1 and #2 go into...
... the TOILET!
This seems a little silly...
WAIT!
I'm not finished!
SPLASH

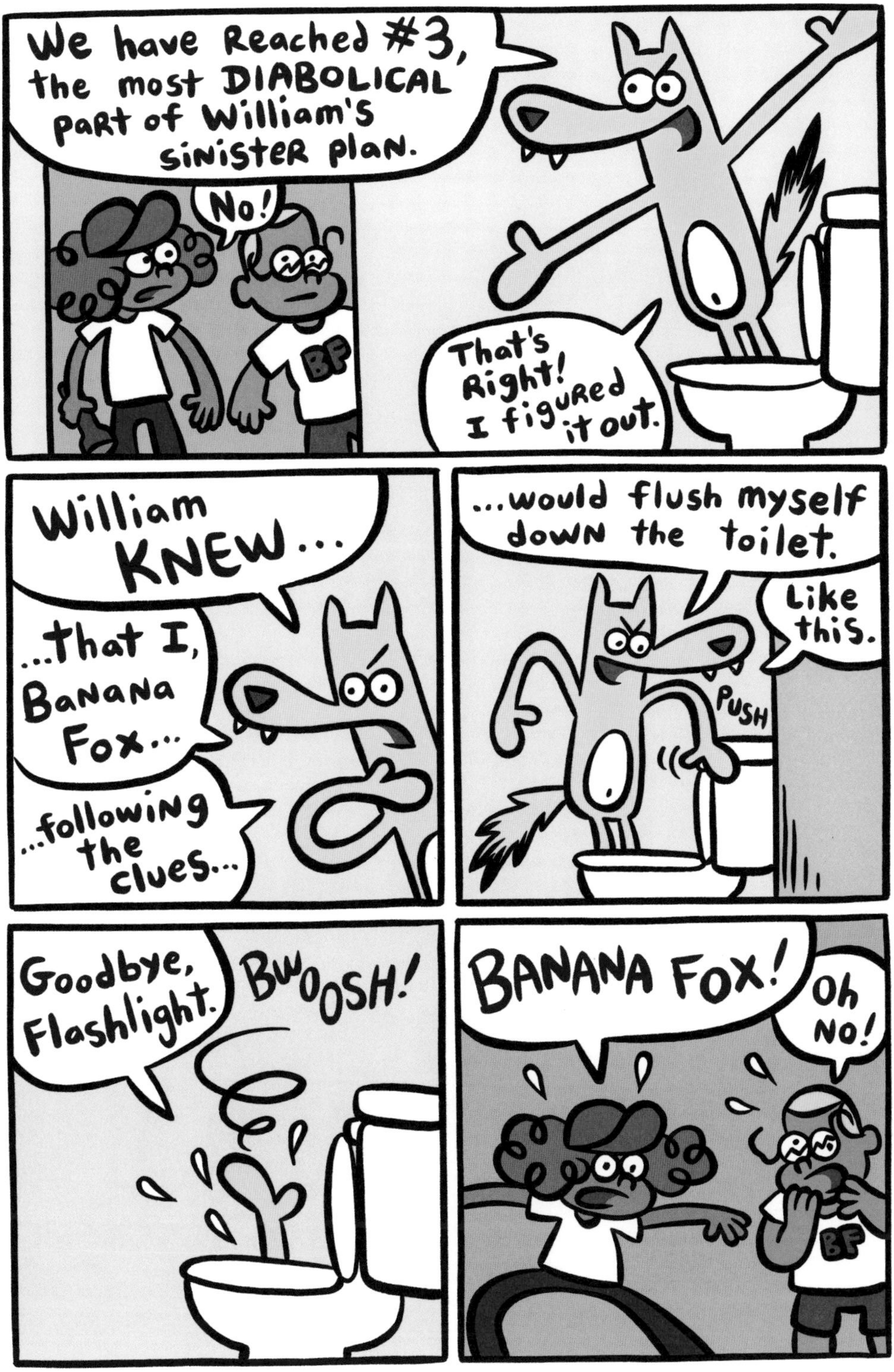
We have Reached #3, the most DIABOLICAL part of William's sinister plan.
No!
That's Right! I figured it out.
William KNEW...
...that I, Banana Fox...
...following the clues...
...would flush myself down the toilet.
Like this.
PUSH
Goodbye, Flashlight.
BWOOOSH!
BANANA FOX!
Oh No!

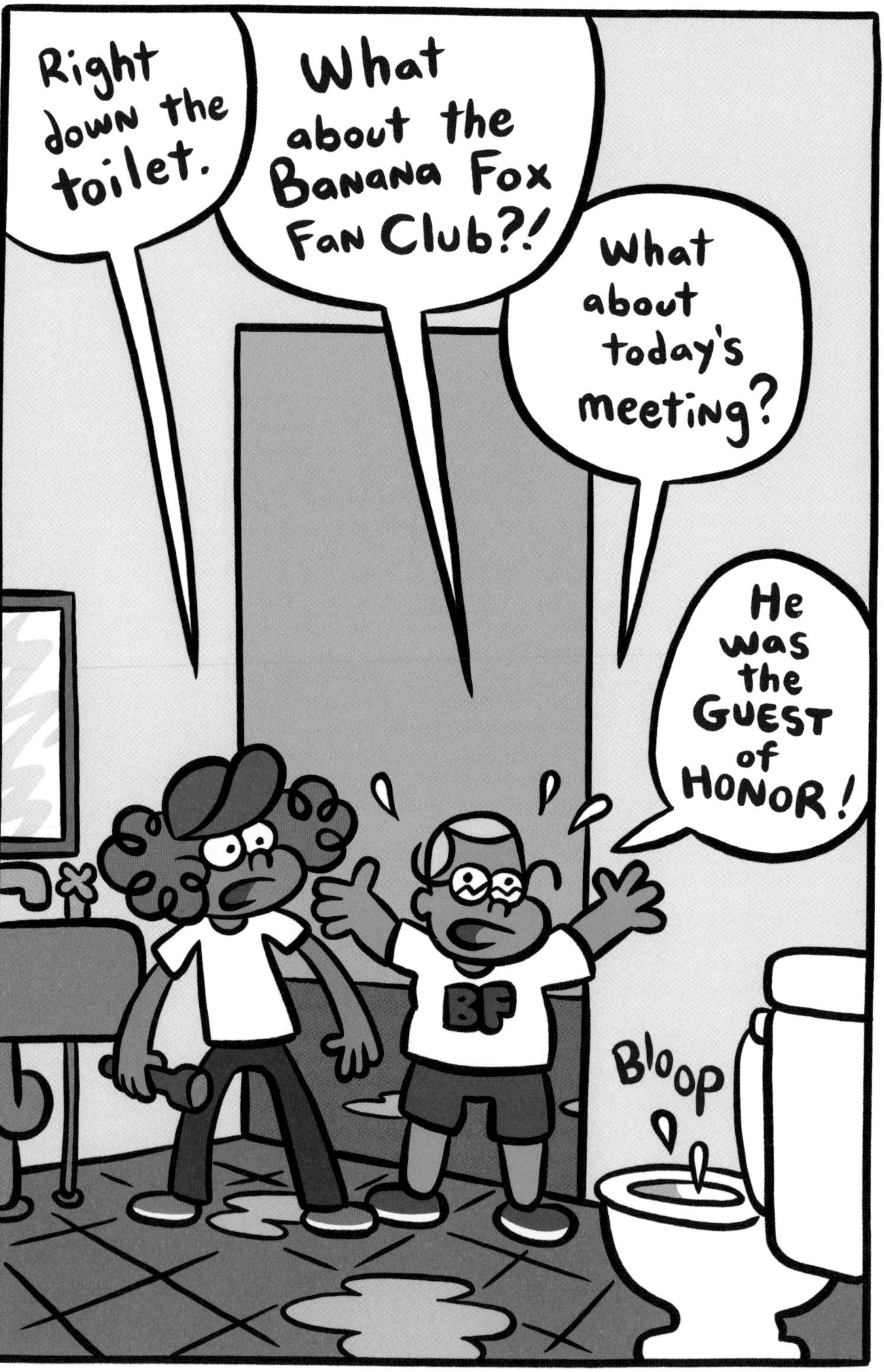
Right down the toilet.
What about the Banana Fox Fan Club?!
What about today's meeting?
He was the GUEST of HONOR!
Bloop
BF

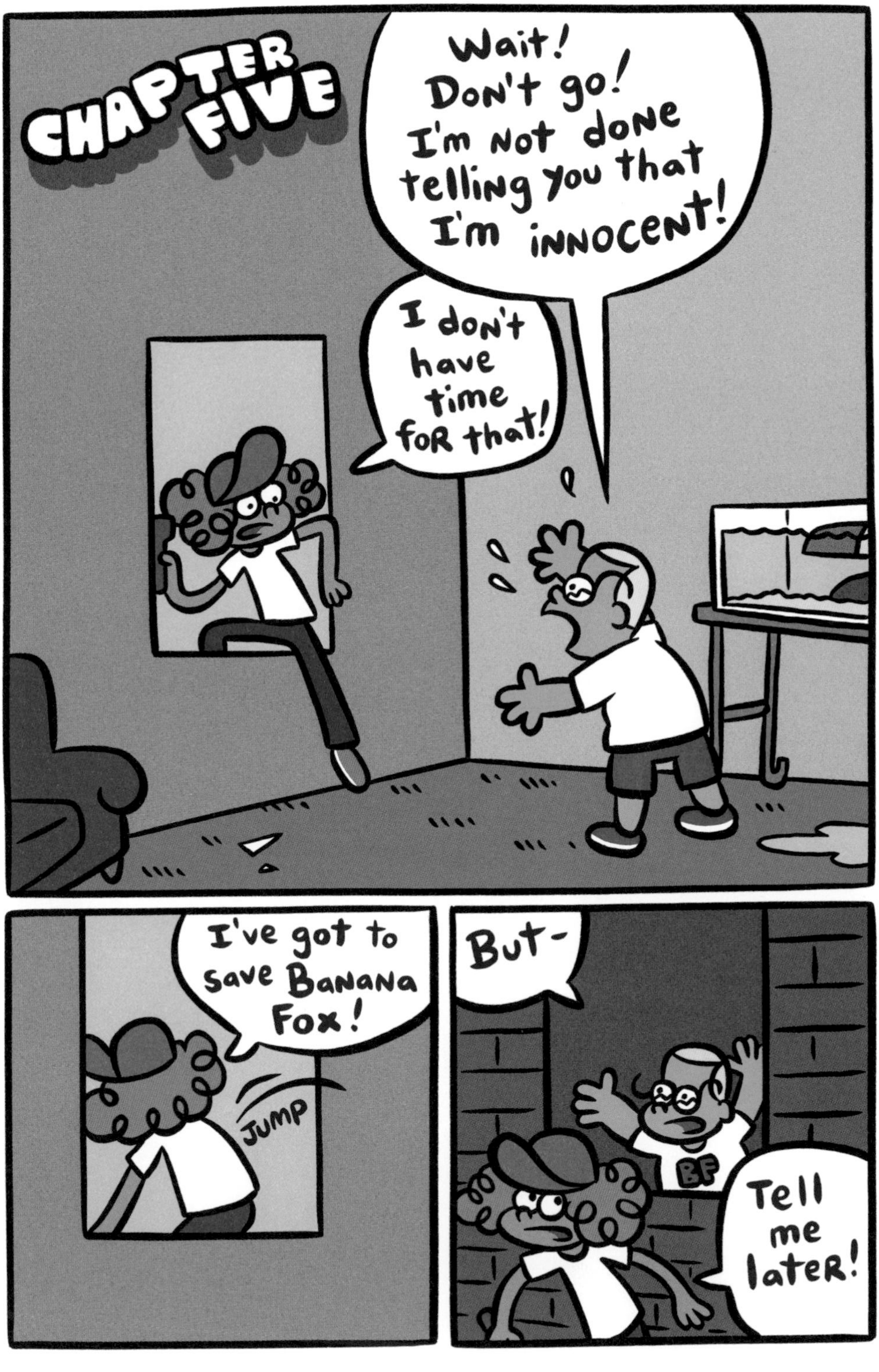
CHAPTER FIVE
Wait! Don't go! I'm not done telling you that I'm INNOCENT!
I don't have time for that!
I've got to save Banana Fox!
JUMP
But-
Tell me later!
BF

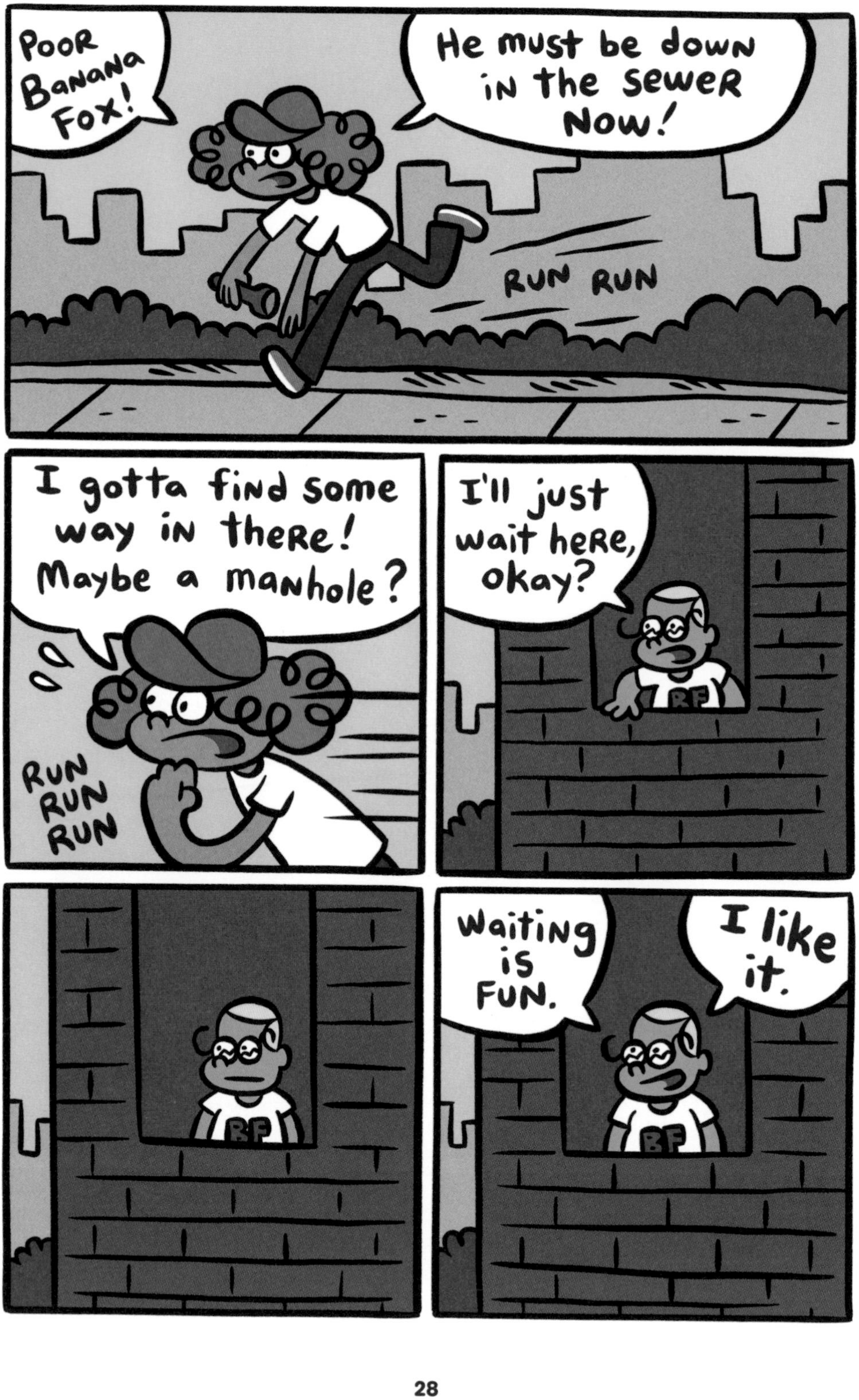
Poor Banana Fox!
He must be down in the sewer now!
RUN RUN
I gotta find some way in there! Maybe a manhole?
RUN RUN RUN
I'll just wait here, okay?
Waiting is fun.
I like it.

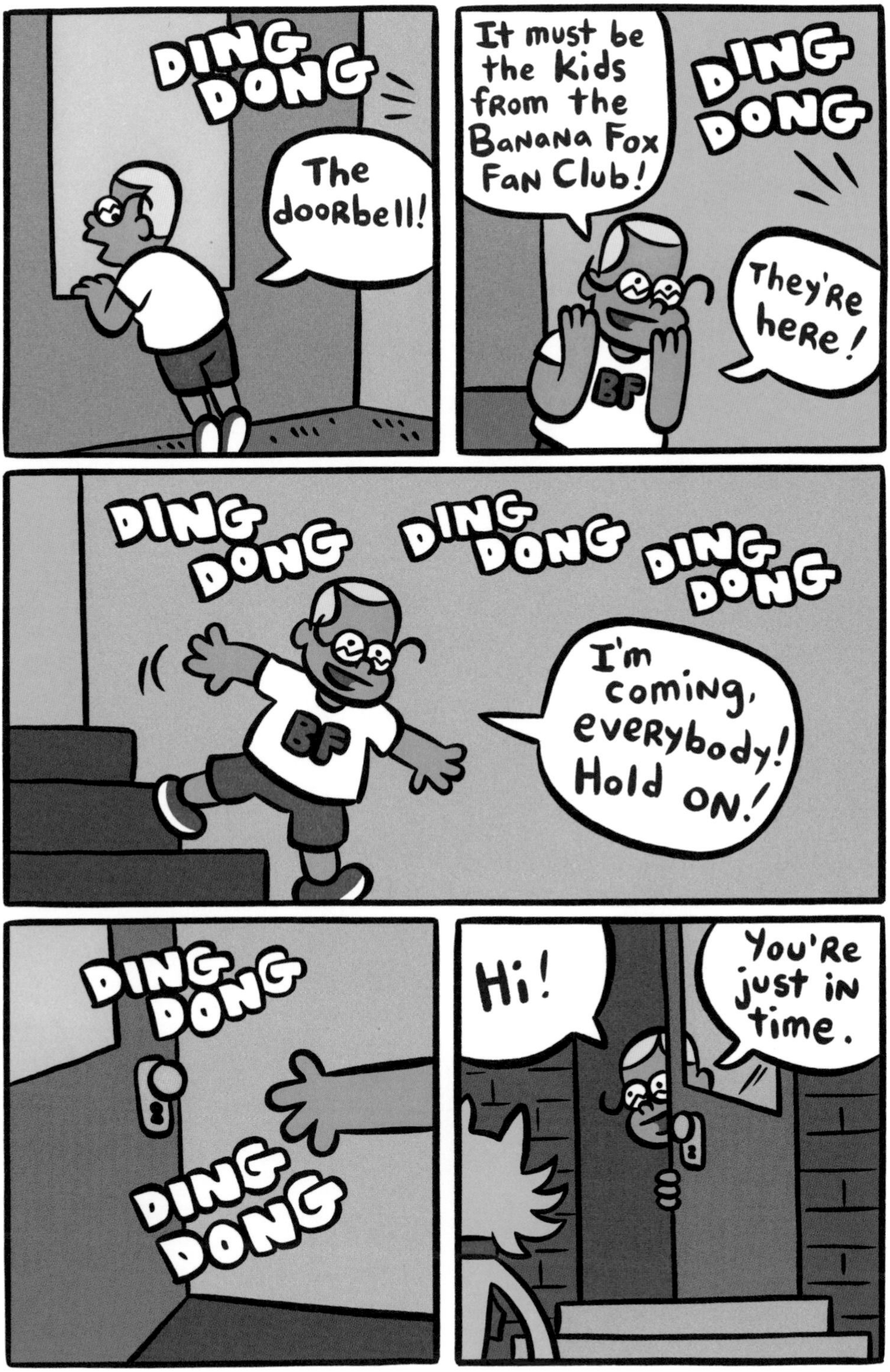
DING DONG
The doorbell!
It must be the Kids from the Banana Fox Fan Club!
DING DONG
They're here!
DING DONG
DING DONG
DING DONG
I'm coming, everybody! Hold ON!
DING DONG
DING DONG
Hi!
You're just in time.

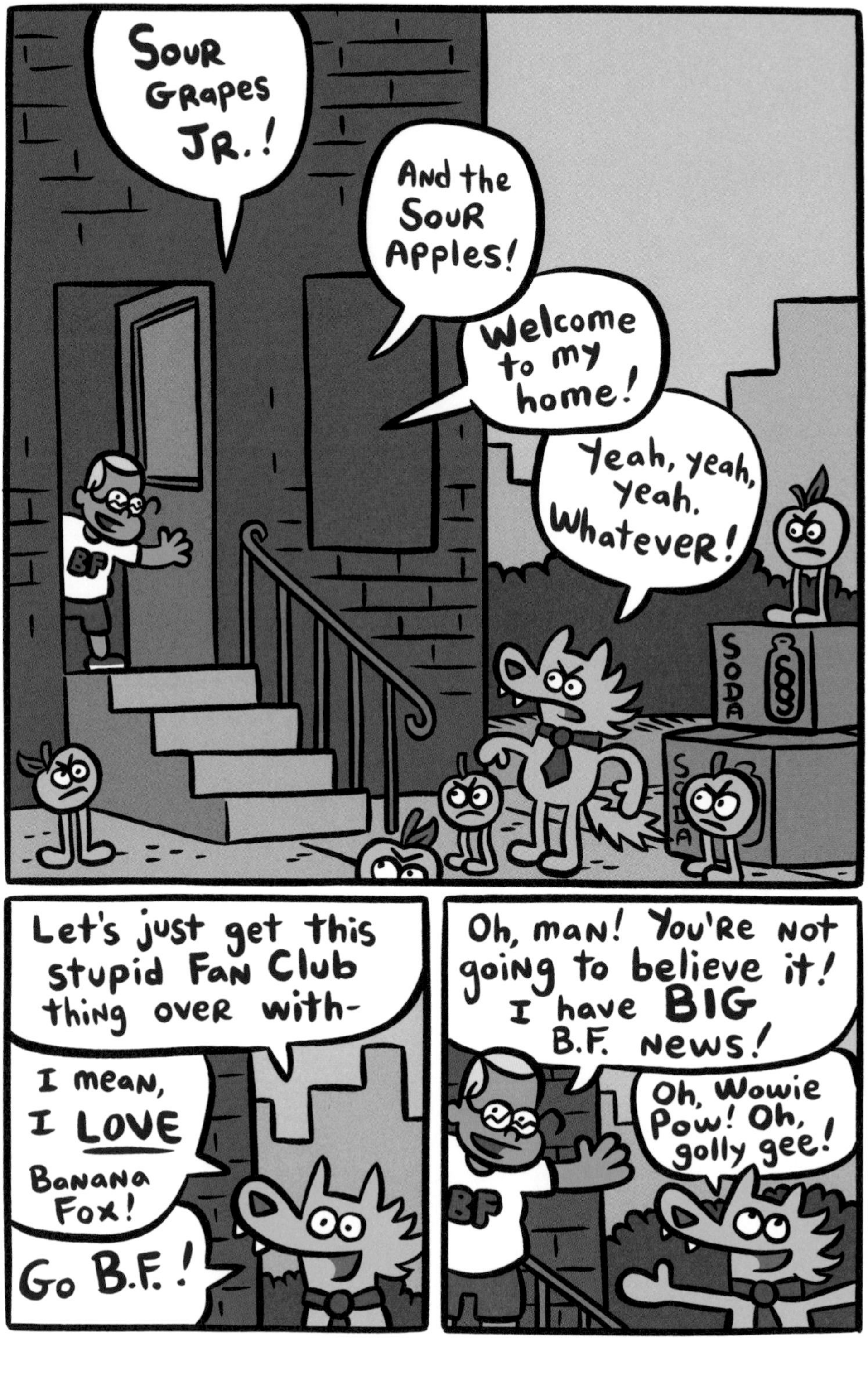
Sour Grapes Jr.!
And the Sour Apples!
Welcome to my home!
Yeah, yeah, yeah. Whatever!
SODA
SODA
Let's just get this stupid Fan Club thing over with-
I mean, I LOVE Banana Fox!
Go B.F.!
Oh, man! You're not going to believe it! I have BIG B.F. news!
Oh, Wowie Pow! Oh, golly gee!

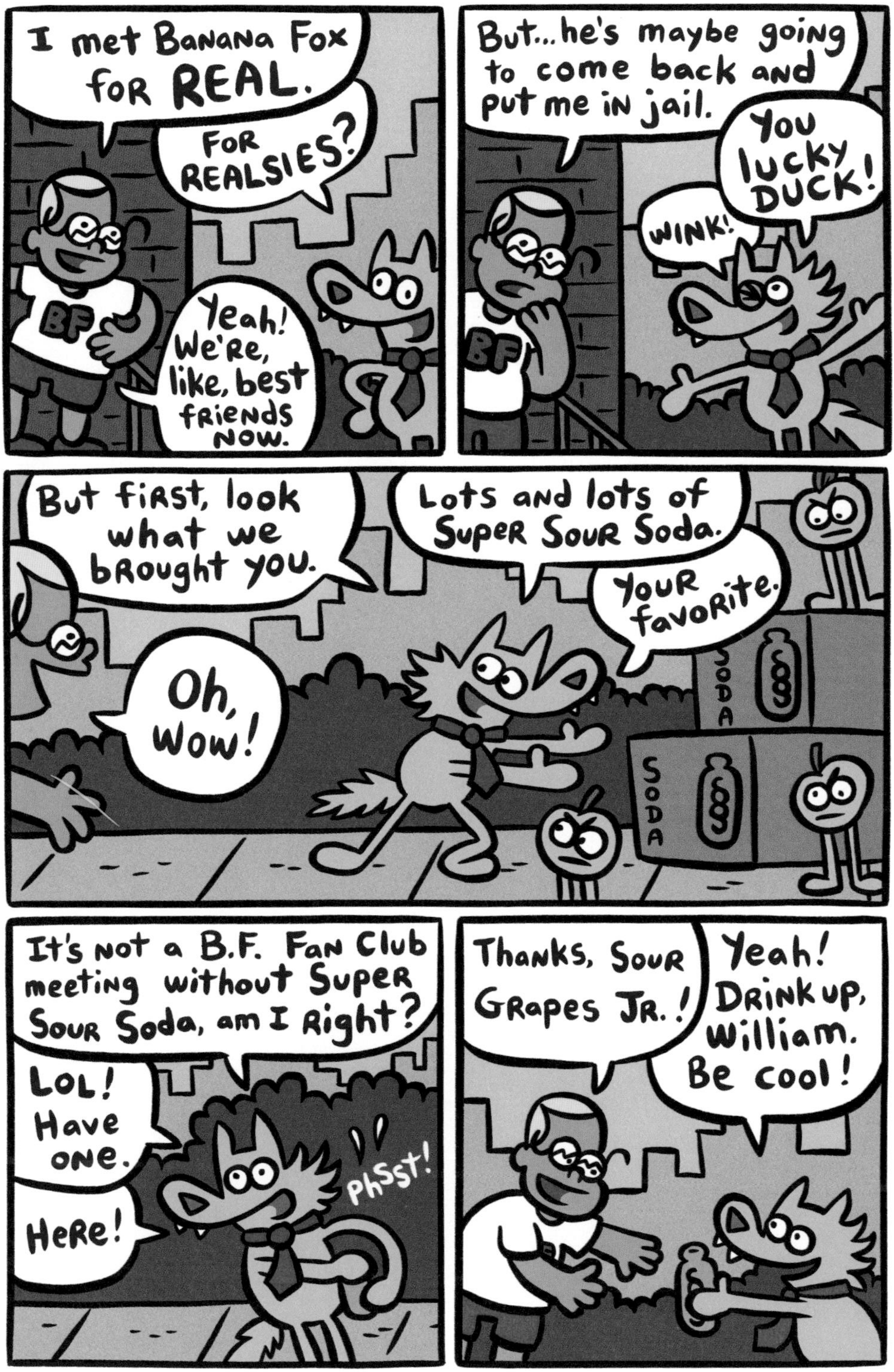
I met Banana Fox for REAL.
FOR REALSIES?
Yeah! We're, like, best friends now.
But... he's maybe going to come back and put me in jail.
You lucky DUCK!
WINK!
But first, look what we brought you.
Lots and lots of Super Sour Soda.
Your favorite.
Oh, wow!
SODA
SODA
It's not a B.F. Fan Club meeting without Super Sour Soda, am I right?
LOL! Have one.
Here!
PhSST!
Thanks, Sour Grapes Jr.!
Yeah! Drink up, William. Be cool!

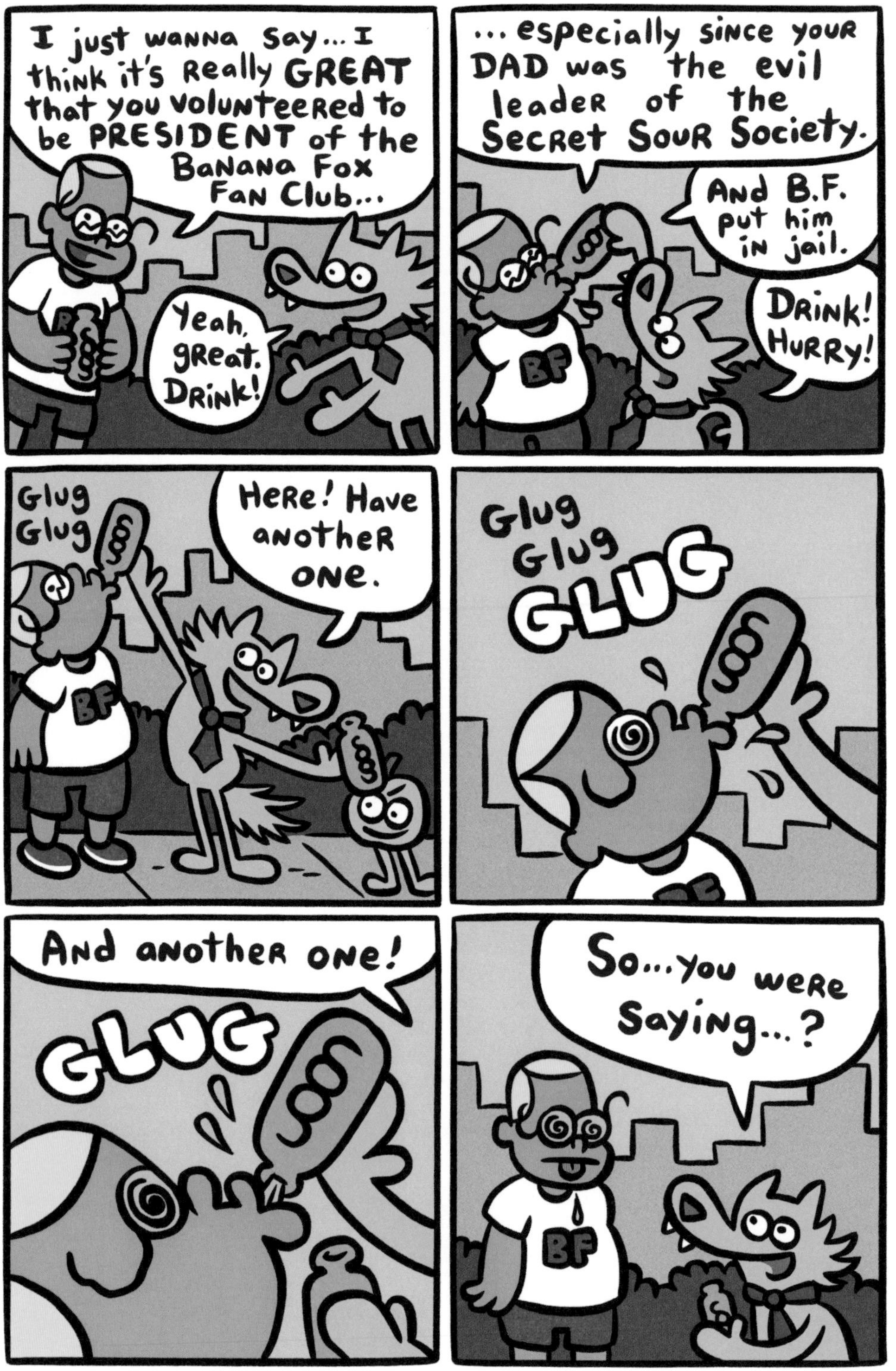
I just wanna say... I think it's Really GREAT that you volunteered to be PRESIDENT of the Banana Fox Fan Club...
Yeah, great. Drink!
...especially since your DAD was the evil leader of the Secret Sour Society.
And B.F. put him in jail.
Drink! Hurry!
Glug Glug
Here! Have another one.
Glug Glug GLUG
And another one!
GLUG
So...you were saying...?

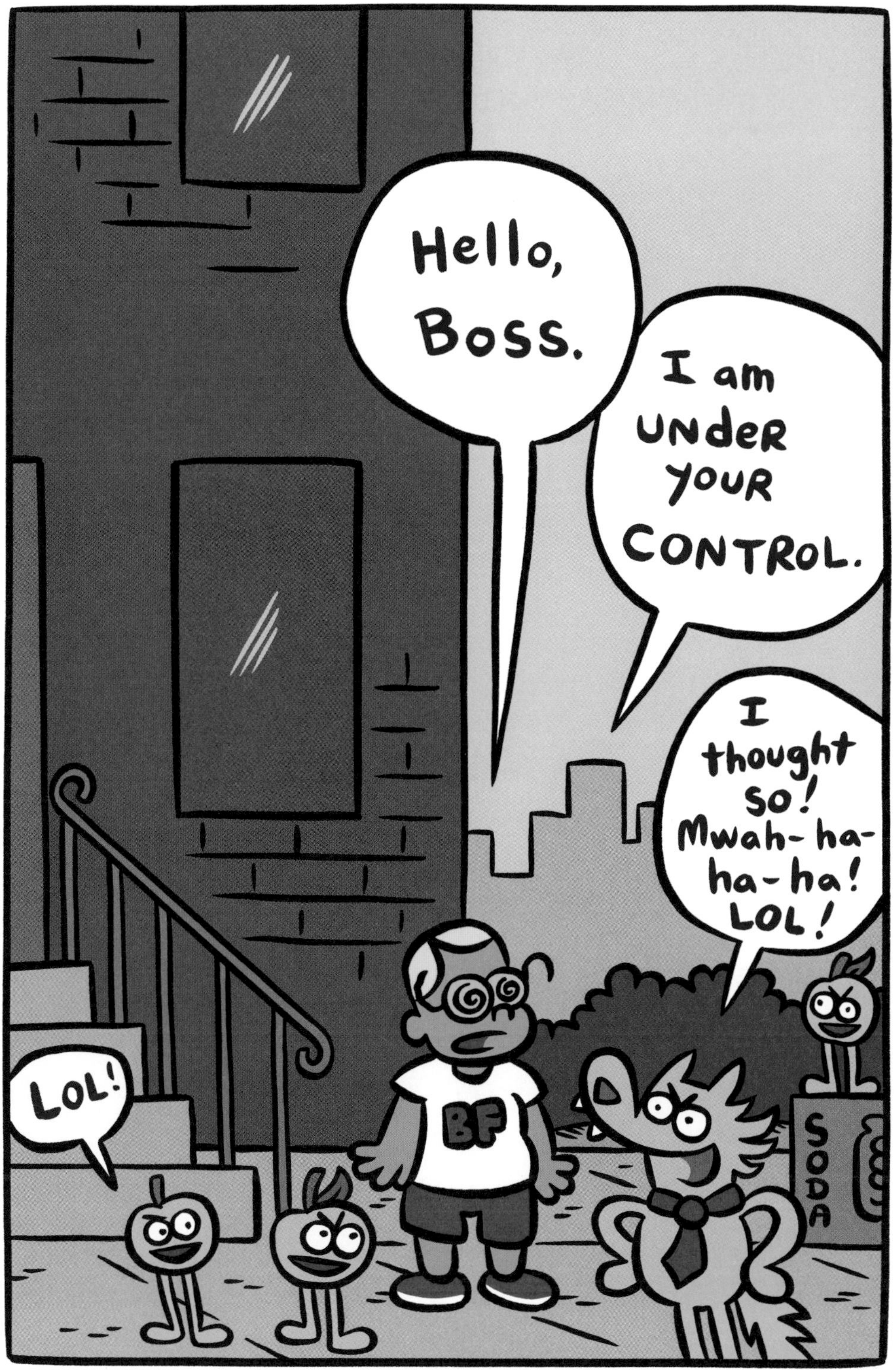
Hello, Boss.
I am UNDER YOUR CONTROL.
I thought so! Mwah-ha-ha-ha! LOL!
LOL!
SODA

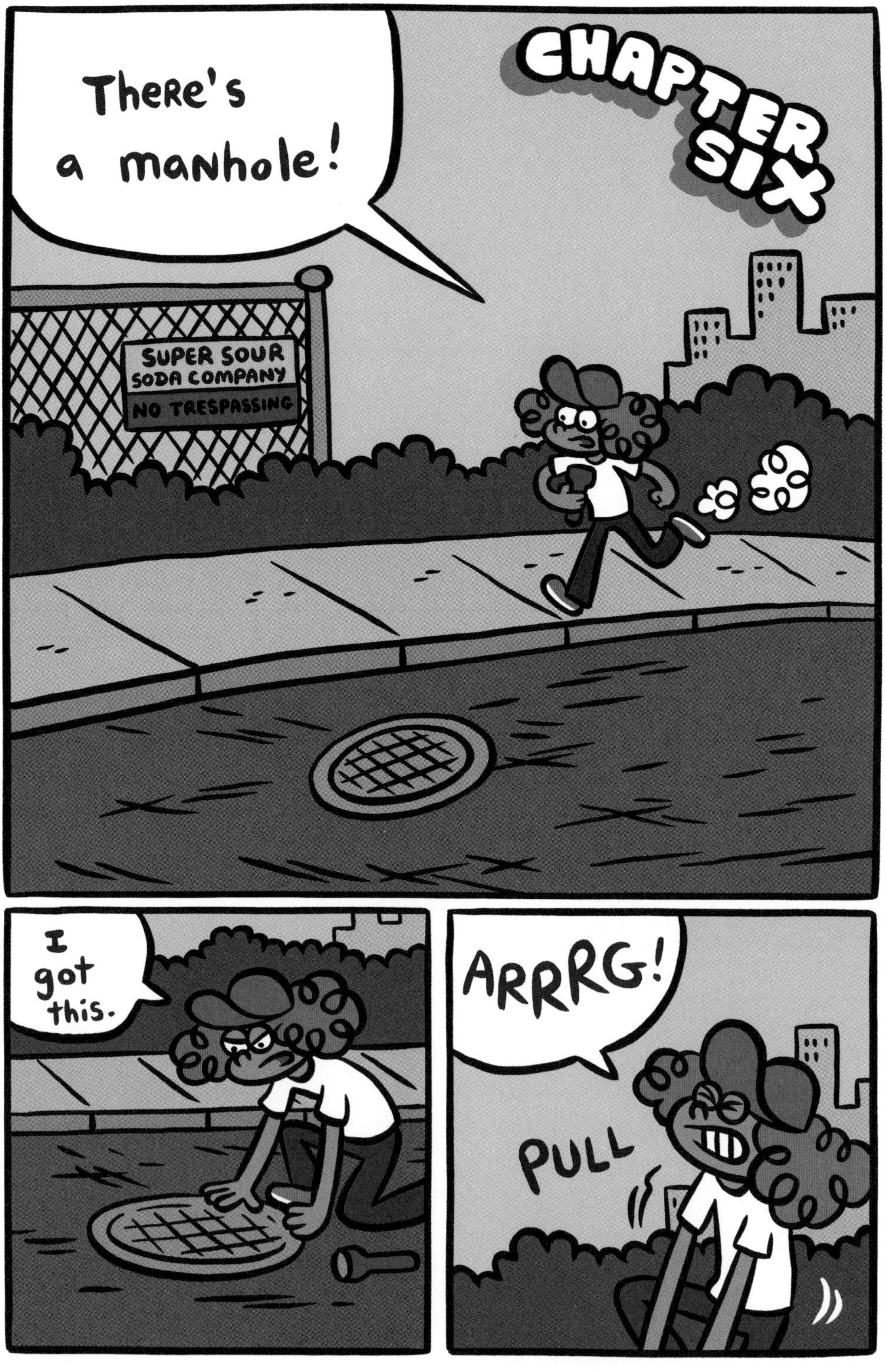
CHAPTER SIX
There's a manhole!
SUPER SOUR SODA COMPANY
NO TRESPASSING
I got this.
ARRRG!
PULL

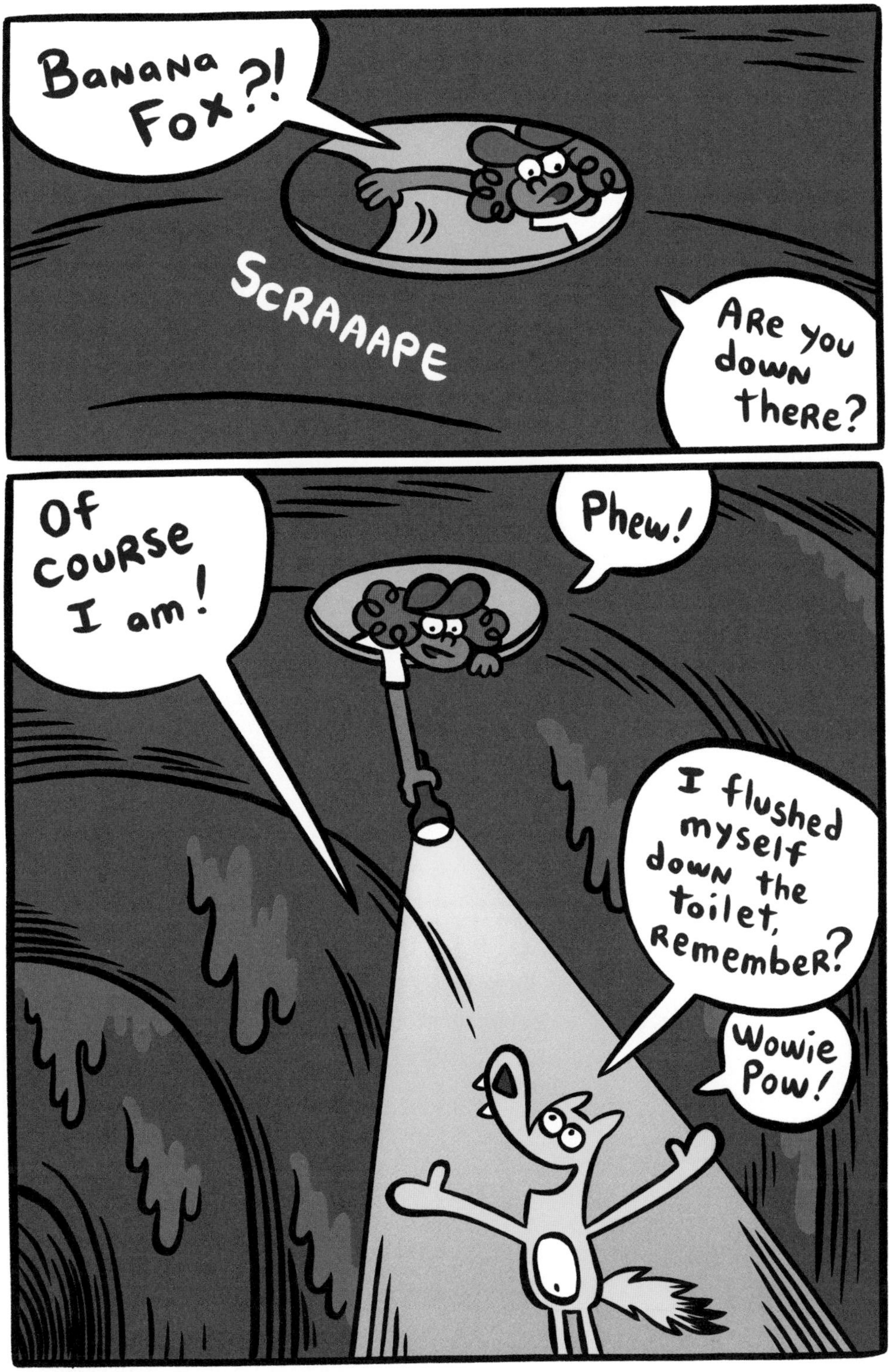
Banana Fox?!
SCRAAAPE
Are you down there?
Of course I am!
Phew!
I flushed myself down the toilet, remember?
Wowie Pow!

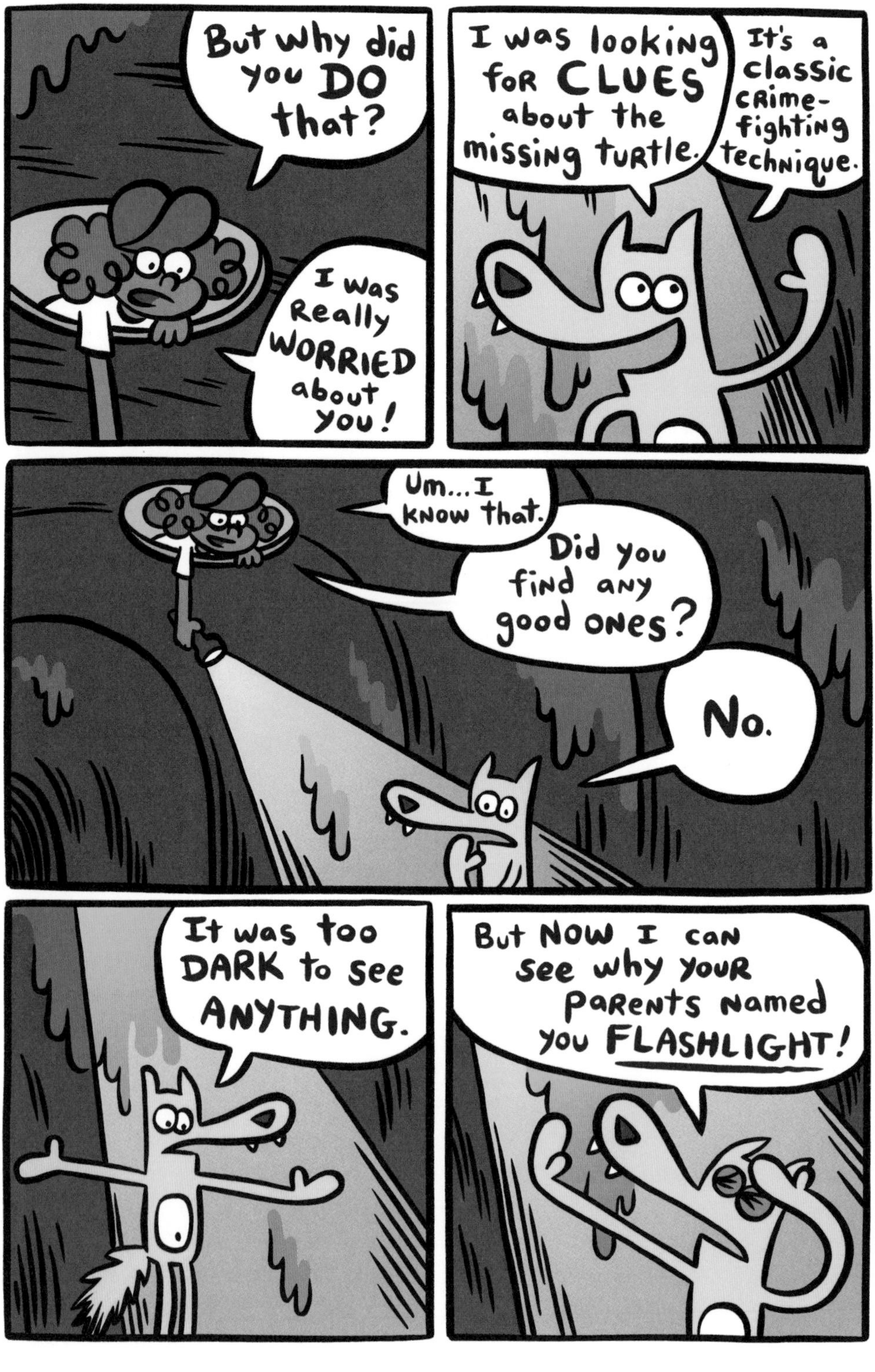
But why did you DO that?
I was really WORRIED about you!
I was looking for CLUES about the missing turtle.
It's a classic crime-fighting technique.
Um... I know that.
Did you find any good ones?
No.
It was too DARK to see ANYTHING.
But NOW I can see why your parents named you FLASHLIGHT!

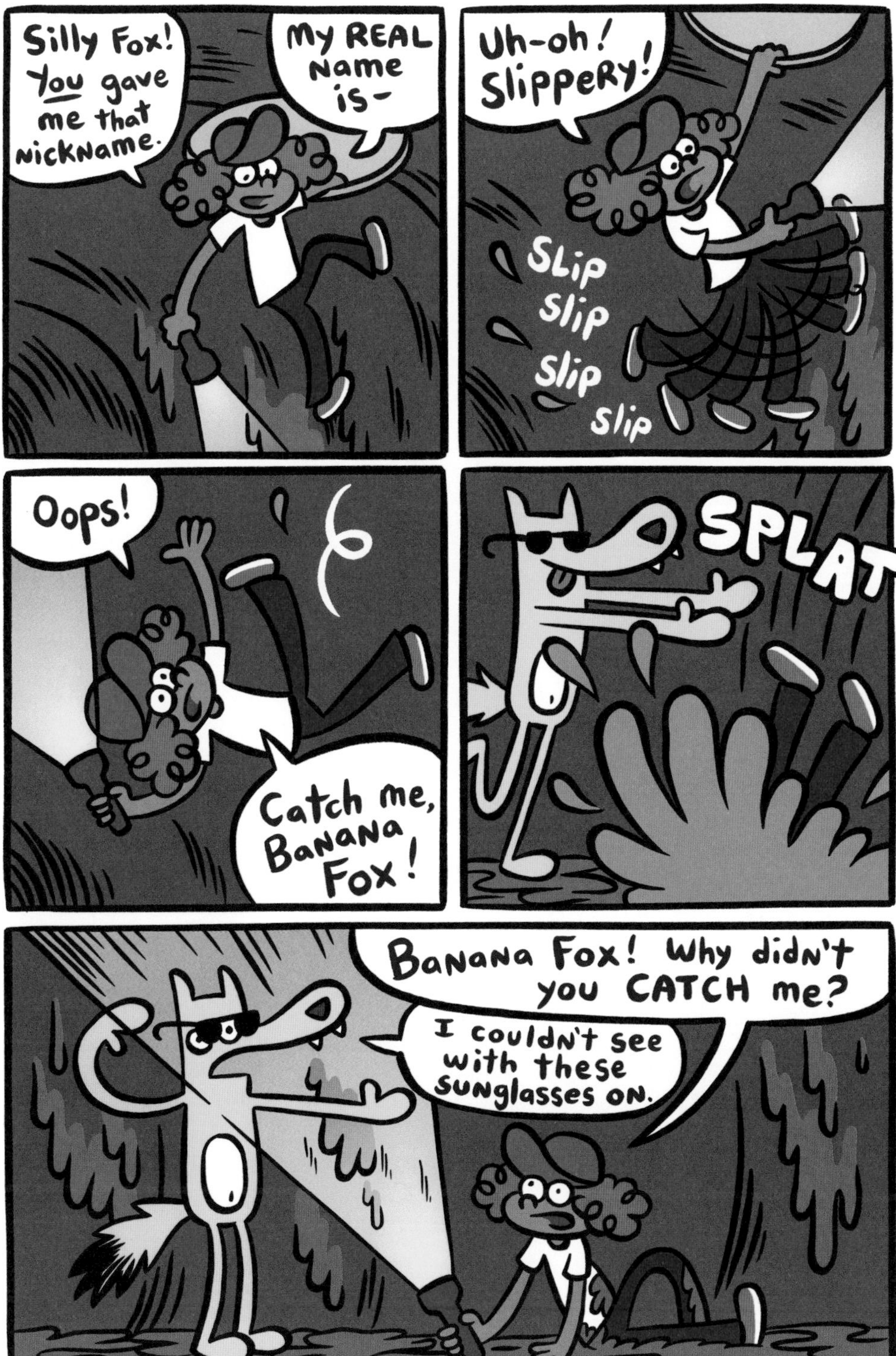
Silly Fox! You gave me that nickname.
My REAL Name is-
Uh-oh! Slippery!
Slip slip slip slip
Oops!
Catch me, Banana Fox!
SPLAT
Banana Fox! Why didn't you CATCH me?
I couldn't see with these sunglasses on.

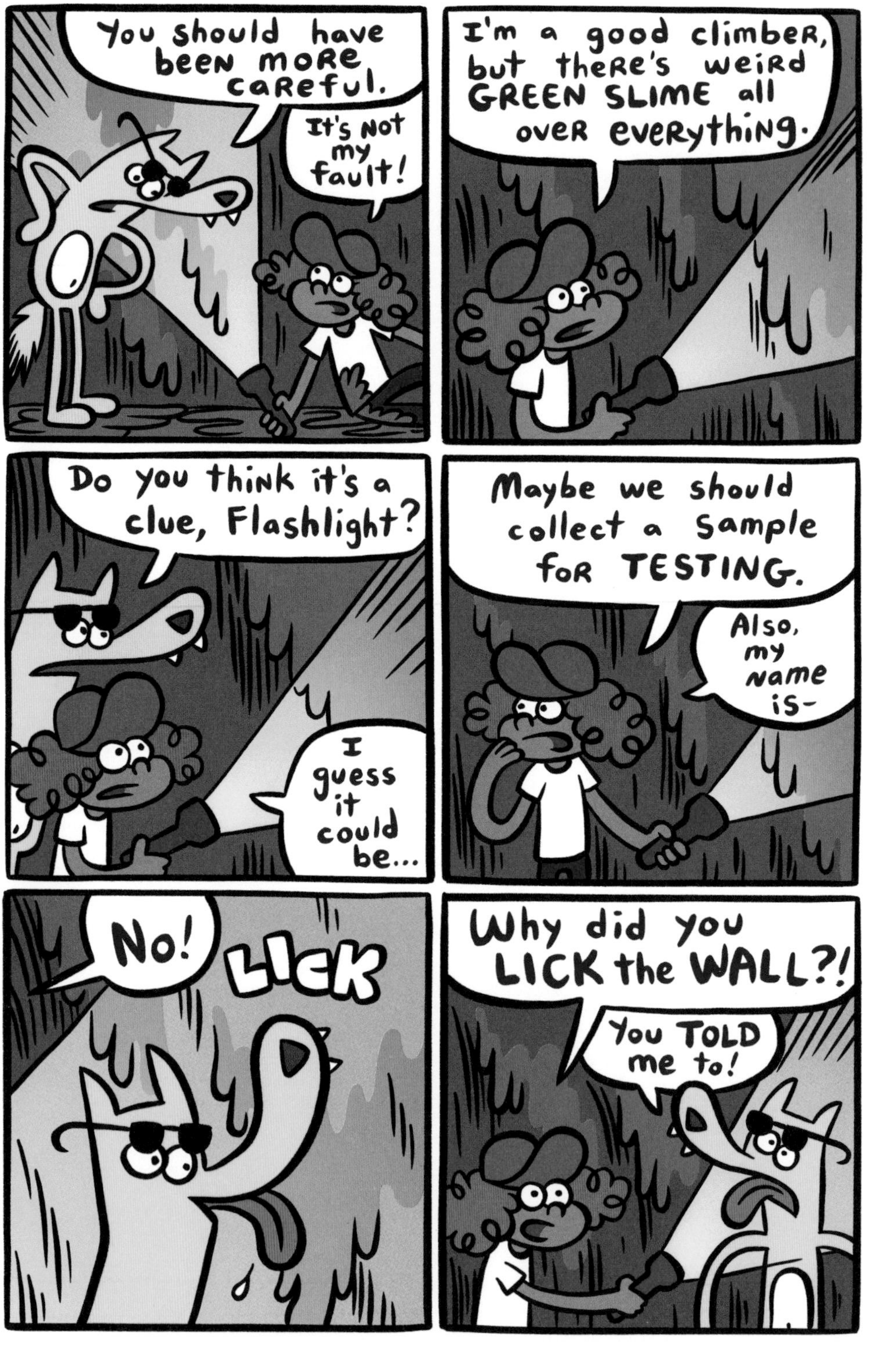
You should have been MORE careful.
It's NOT my fault!
I'm a good climber, but there's weird GREEN SLIME all over everything.
Do you think it's a clue, Flashlight?
I guess it could be...
Maybe we should collect a sample for TESTING.
Also, my name is-
No!
LICK
Why did you LICK the WALL?!
You TOLD me to!

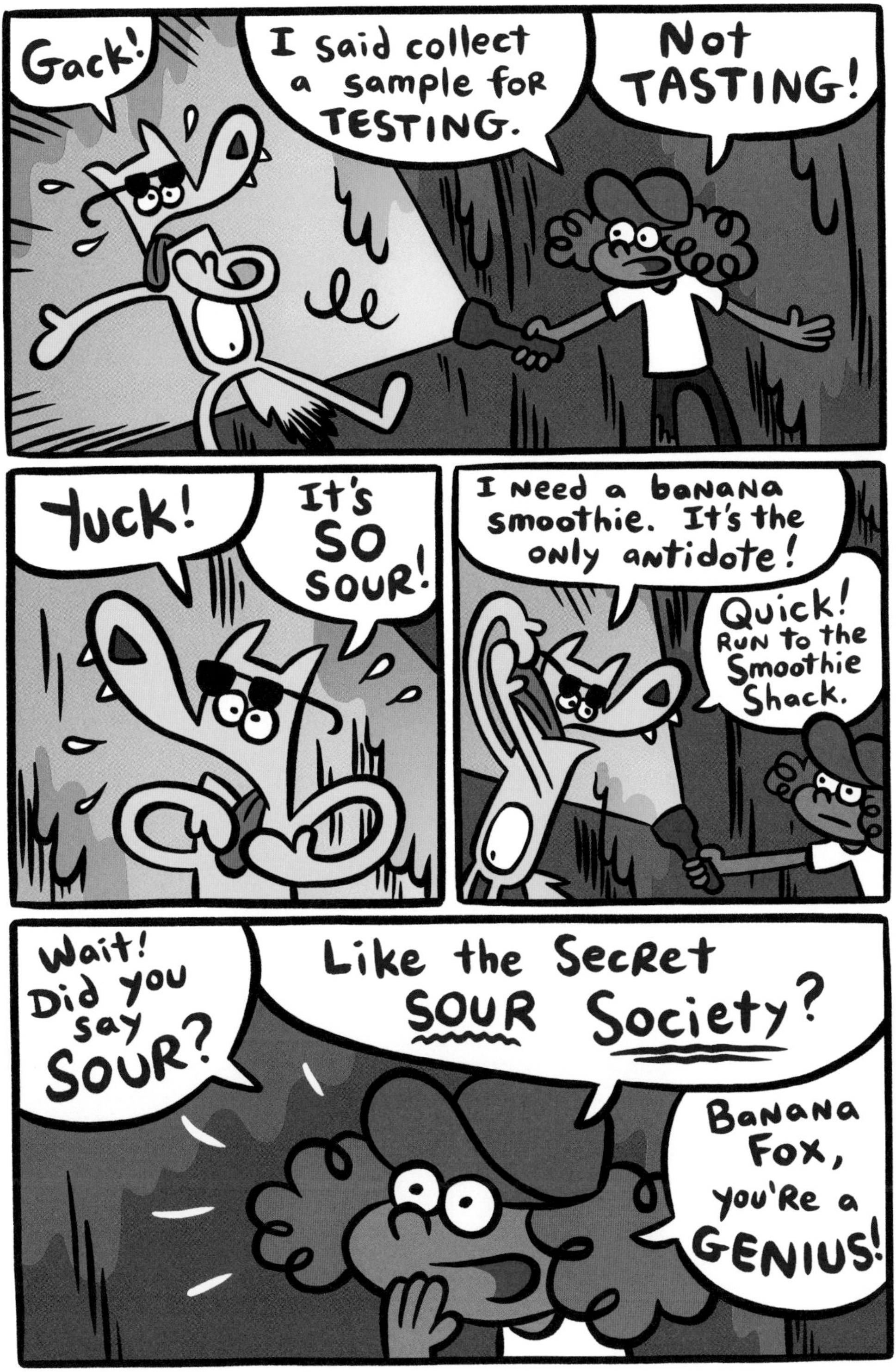
Gack!
I said collect a sample for TESTING.
Not TASTING!
Yuck!
It's SO SOUR!
I need a banana smoothie. It's the only antidote!
Quick! Run to the Smoothie Shack.
Wait! Did you say SOUR?
Like the Secret SOUR Society?
Banana Fox, you're a GENIUS!

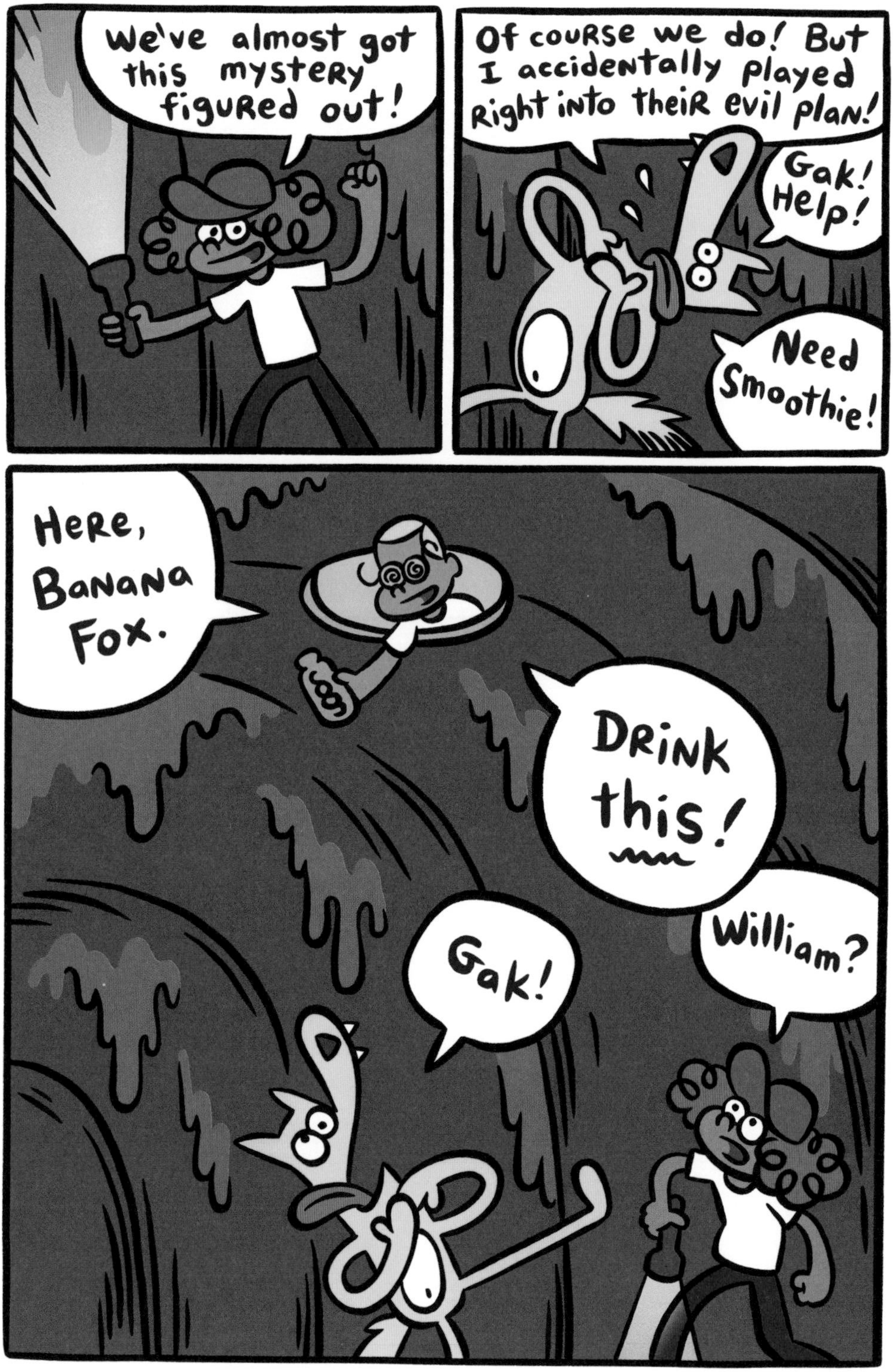
We've almost got this mystery figured out!
Of course we do! But I accidentally played right into their evil plan!
Gak! Help!
Need Smoothie!
Here, Banana Fox.
Drink this!
Gak!
William?

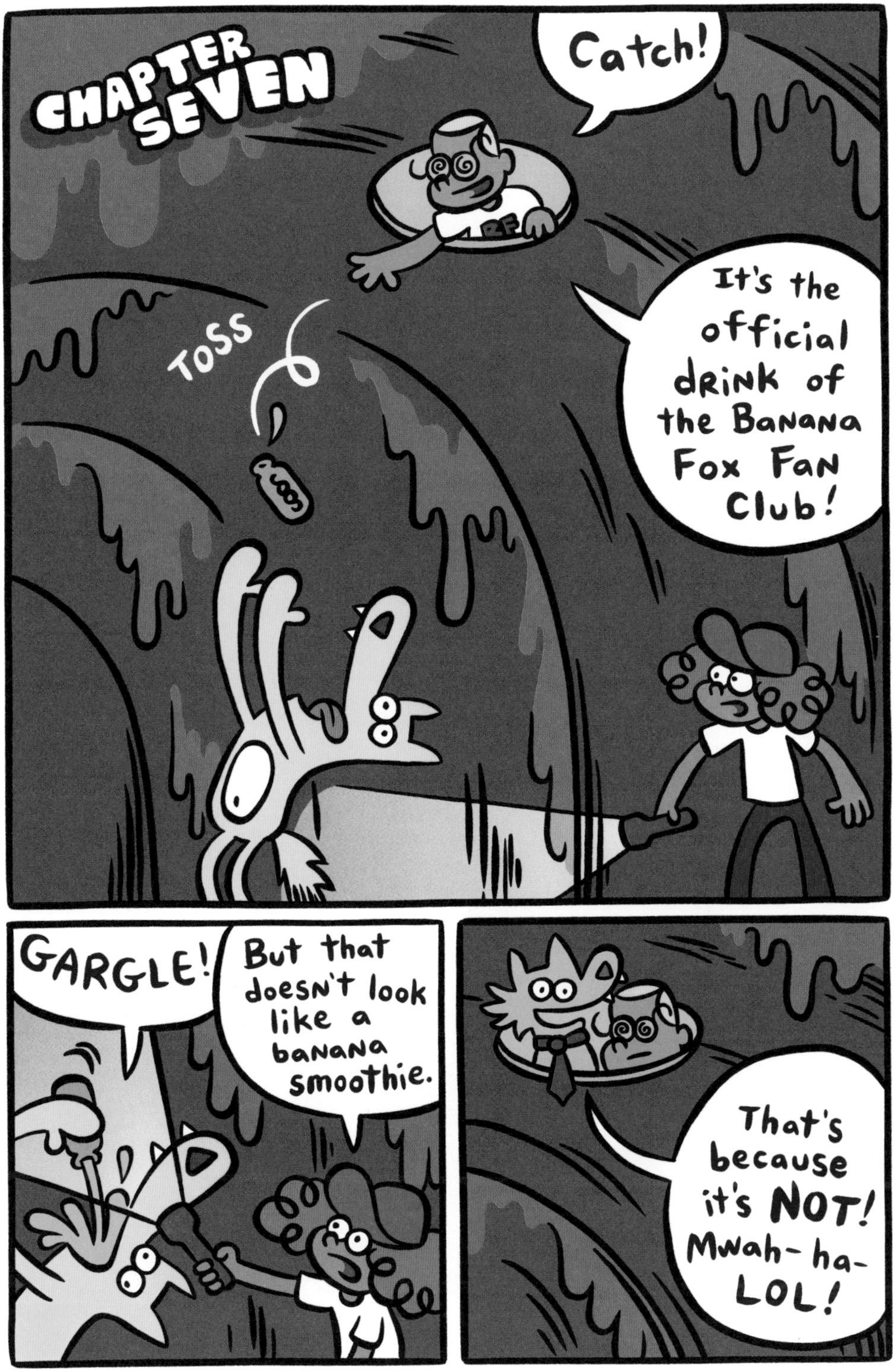
CHAPTER SEVEN
Catch!
It's the official drink of the Banana Fox Fan Club!
TOSS
GARGLE!
But that doesn't look like a banana smoothie.
That's because it's NOT! Mwah-ha-LOL!

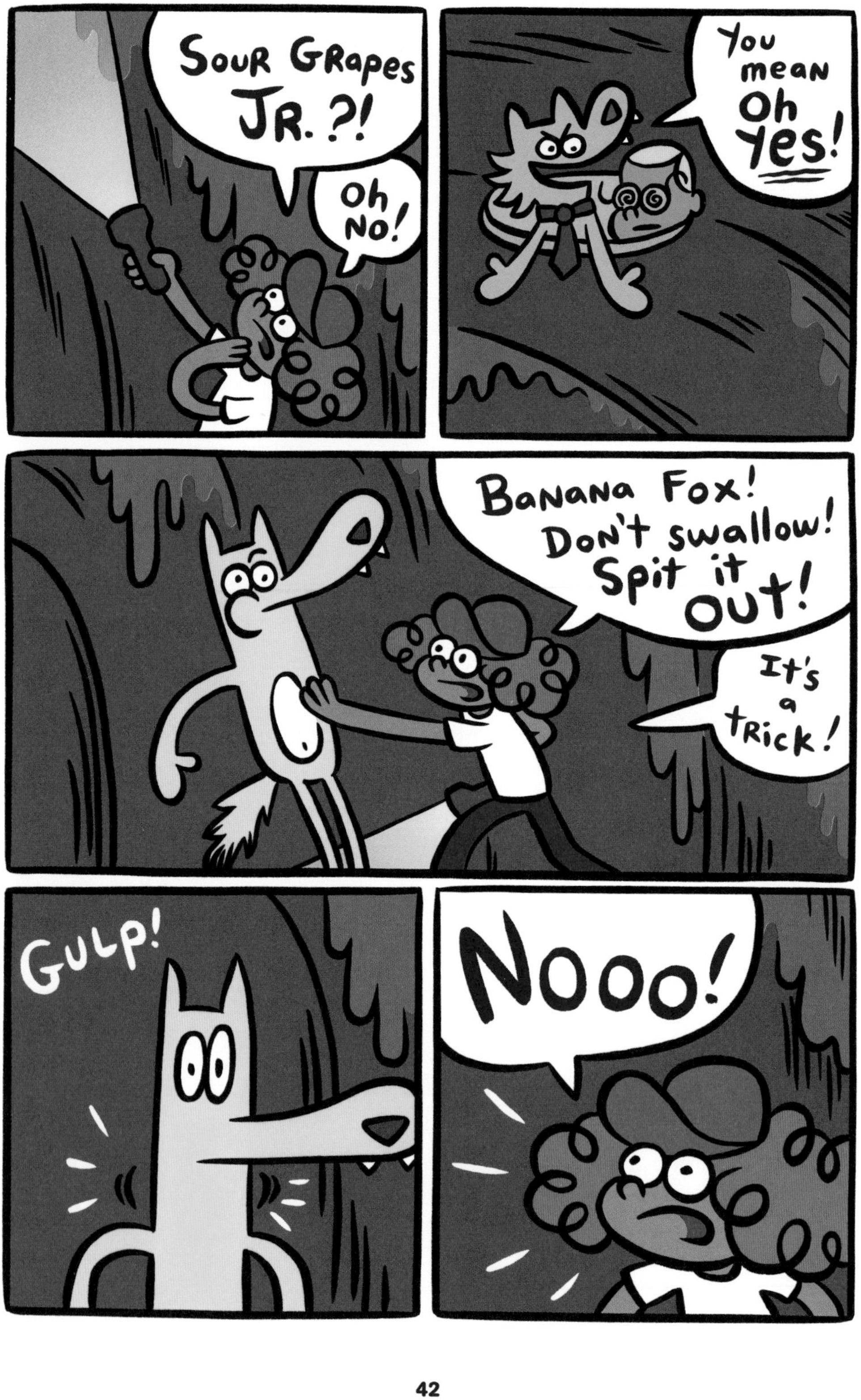
Sour Grapes JR.?!
Oh No!
You mean Oh Yes!
Banana Fox! Don't swallow! Spit it OUT!
It's a trick!
GULP!
NOOO!

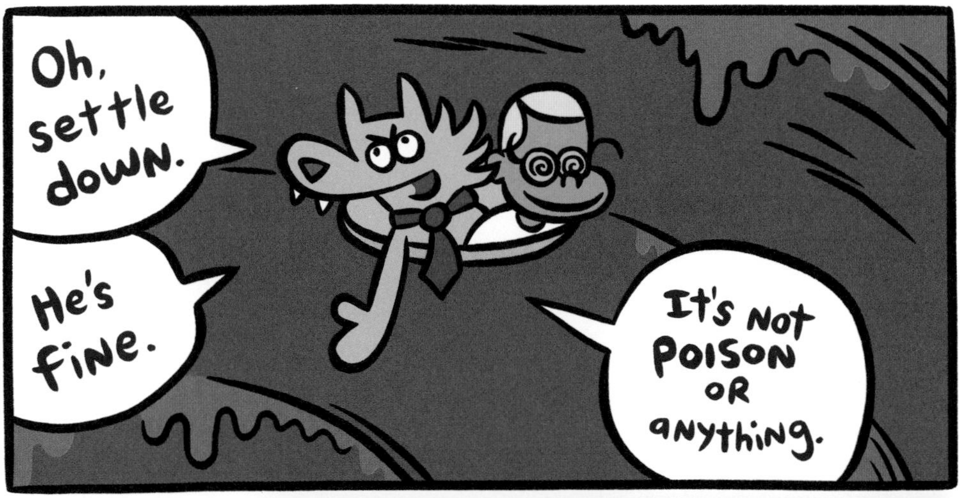
Oh, settle down.
He's fine.
It's not POISON OR anything.

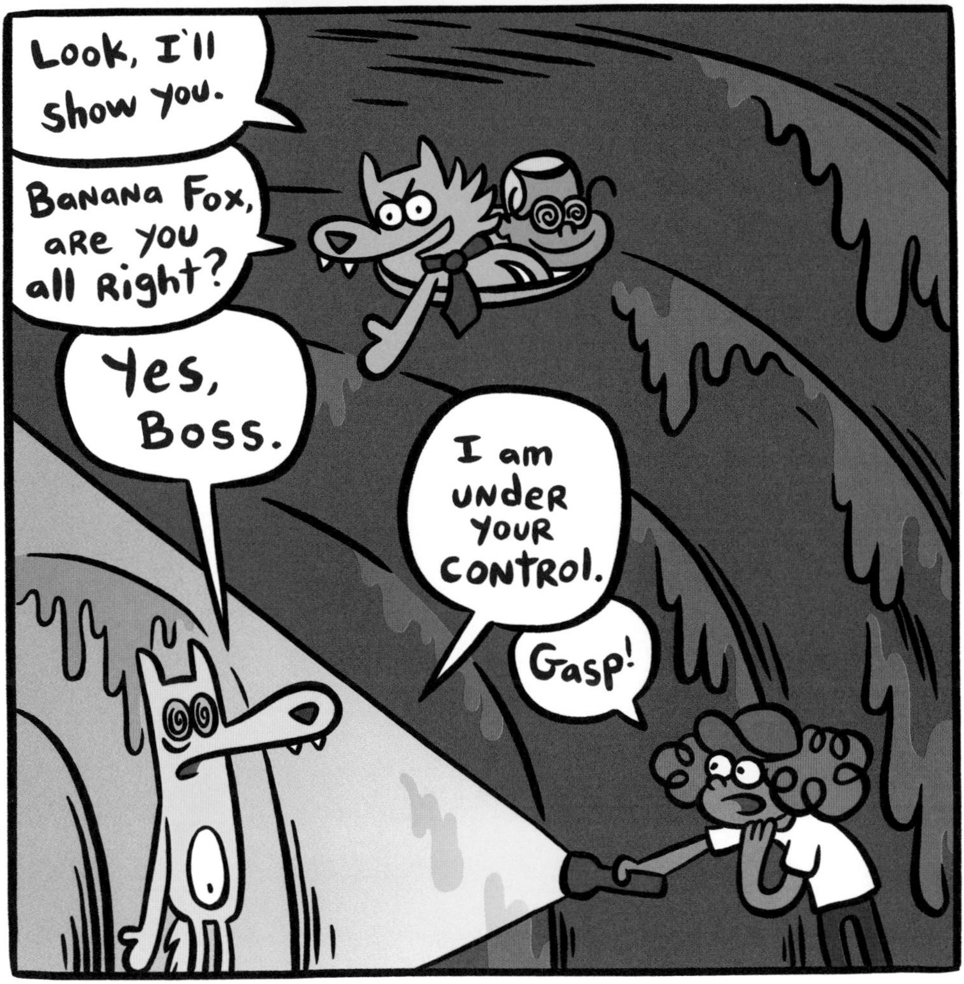
Look, I'll show you.
Banana Fox, are you all Right?
Yes, Boss.
I am under your control.
Gasp!

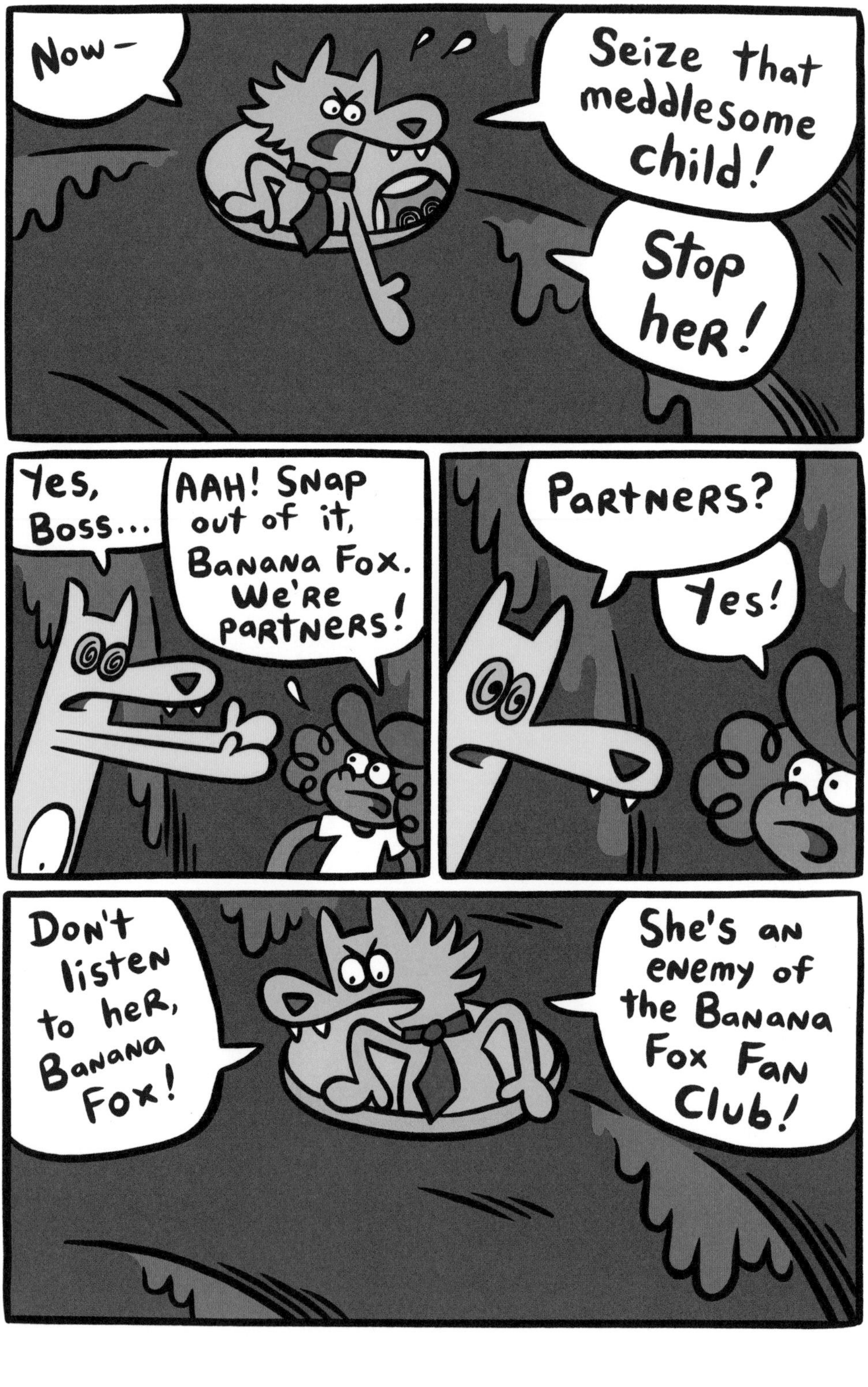

Now-
Seize that meddlesome child!
Stop her!
Yes, Boss...
AAH! Snap out of it, Banana Fox. We're partners!
Partners?
Yes!
Don't listen to her, Banana Fox!
She's an enemy of the Banana Fox Fan Club!

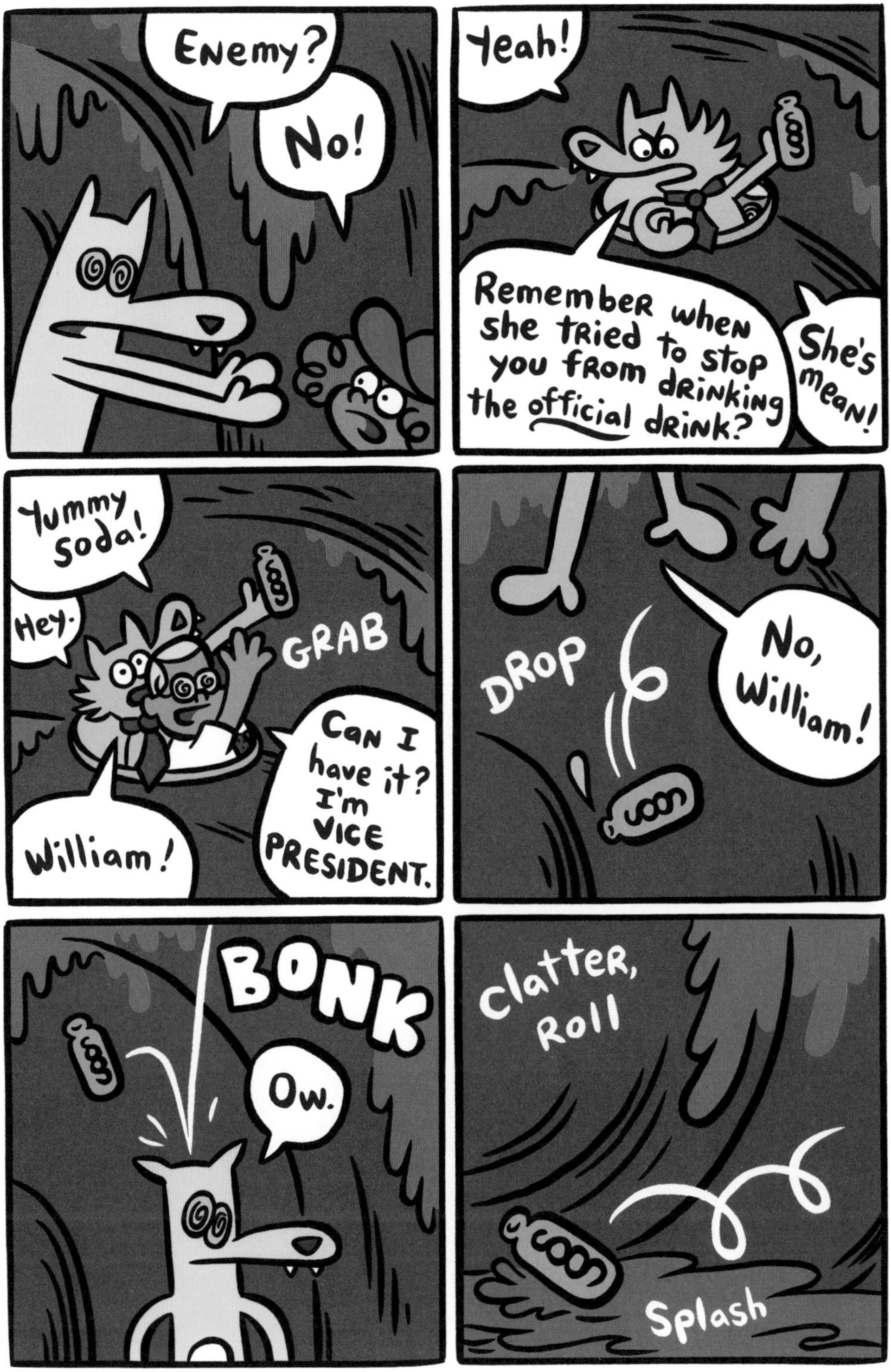
Enemy?
No!
Yeah!
Remember when she tried to stop you from drinking the official drink?
She's mean!
Yummy soda!
Hey.
GRAB
William!
Can I have it? I'm VICE PRESIDENT.
DROP
No, William!
BONK
Ow.
Clatter, Roll
Splash

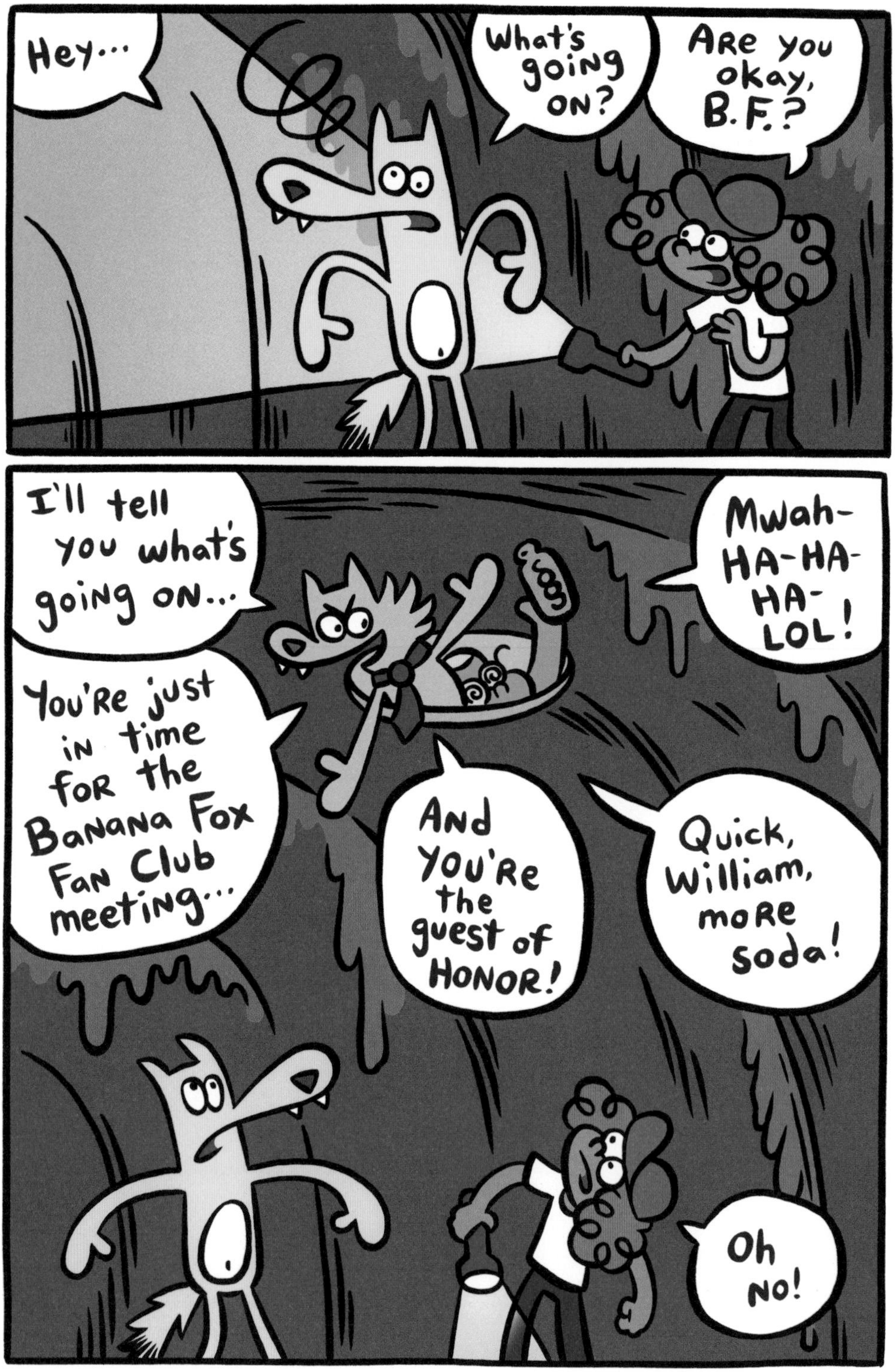
Hey...
What's going on?
Are you okay, B.F.?
I'll tell you what's going on...
Mwah-HA-HA-HA-LOL!
You're just in time for the Banana Fox Fan Club meeting...
And YOU'RE the guest of HONOR!
Quick, William, more soda!
Oh No!

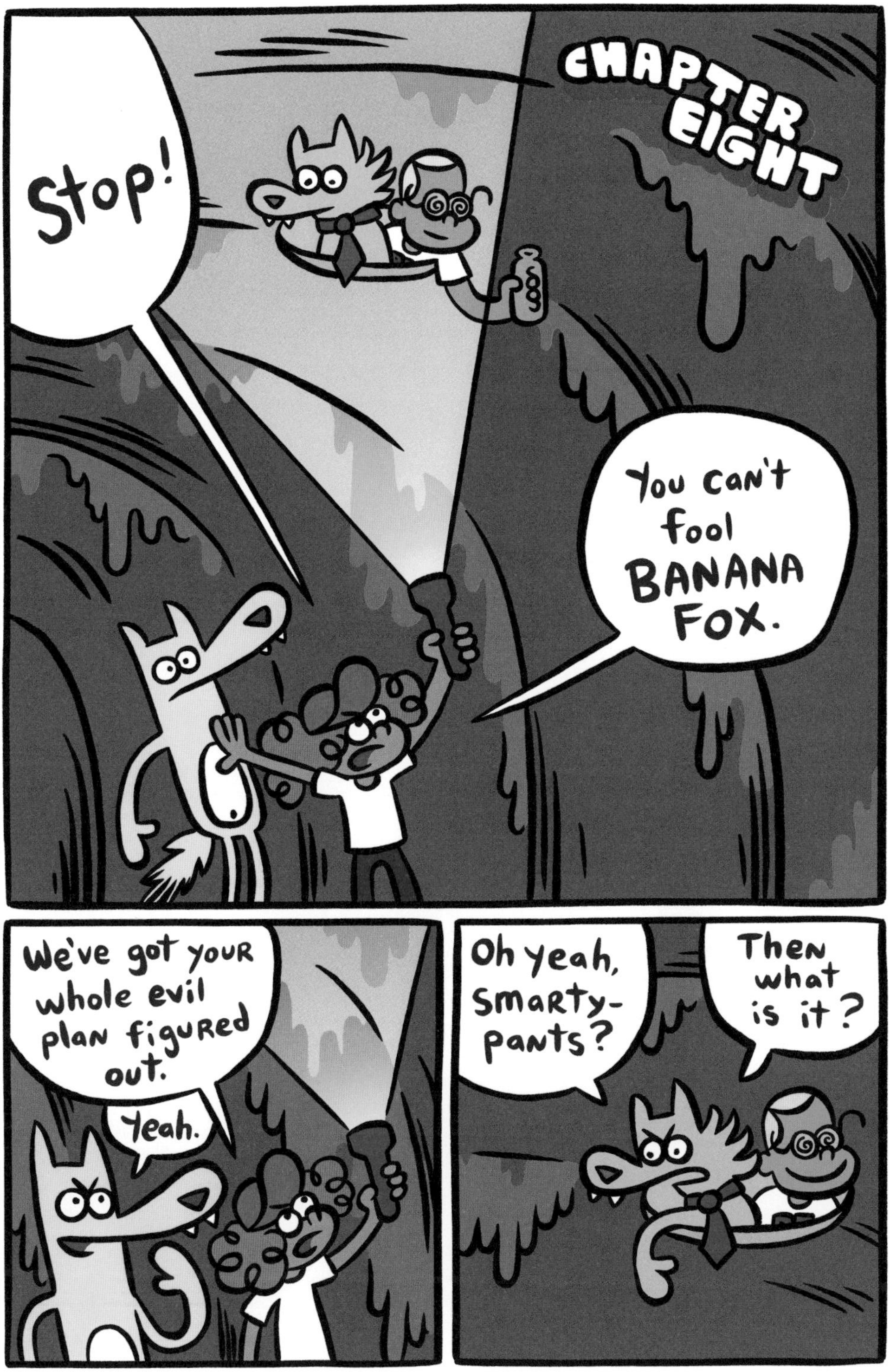
CHAPTER EIGHT
Stop!
You can't fool BANANA FOX.
We've got your whole evil plan figured out.
Yeah.
Oh yeah, smarty-pants?
Then what is it?

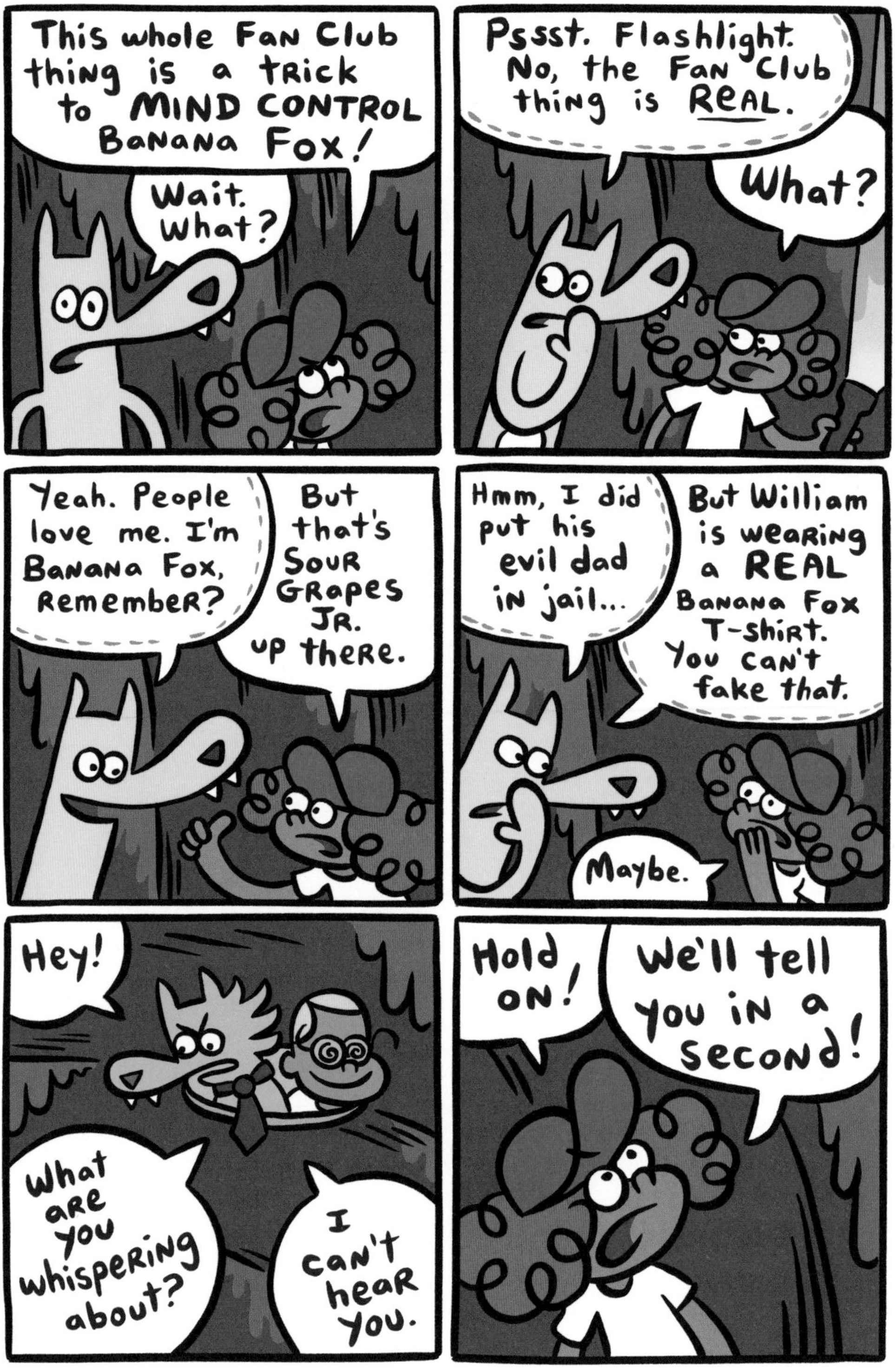

This whole Fan Club thing is a trick to MIND CONTROL Banana Fox!
Wait. What?
Pssst. Flashlight. No, the Fan Club thing is REAL.
What?
Yeah. People love me. I'm Banana Fox, remember?
But that's Sour Grapes Jr. up there.
Hmm, I did put his evil dad in jail...
But William is wearing a REAL Banana Fox T-shirt. You can't fake that.
Maybe.
Hey!
What are you whispering about?
I can't hear you.
Hold on!
We'll tell you in a second!

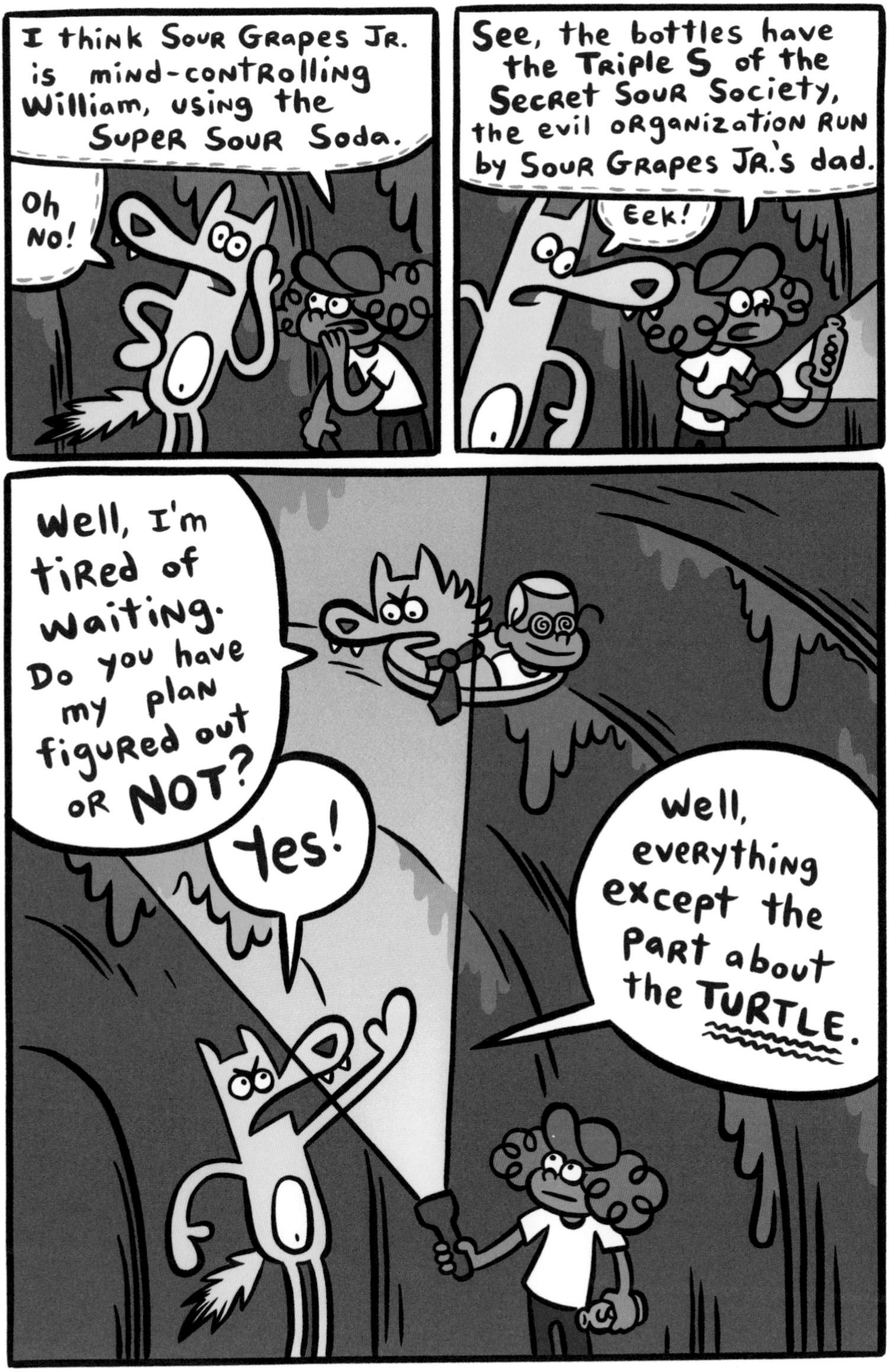
I think Sour Grapes Jr. is mind-controlling William, using the Super Sour Soda.
Oh No!
See, the bottles have the Triple S of the Secret Sour Society, the evil organization run by Sour Grapes Jr.'s dad.
Eek!
Well, I'm tired of waiting. Do you have my plan figured out or NOT?
Yes!
Well, everything except the part about the TURTLE.

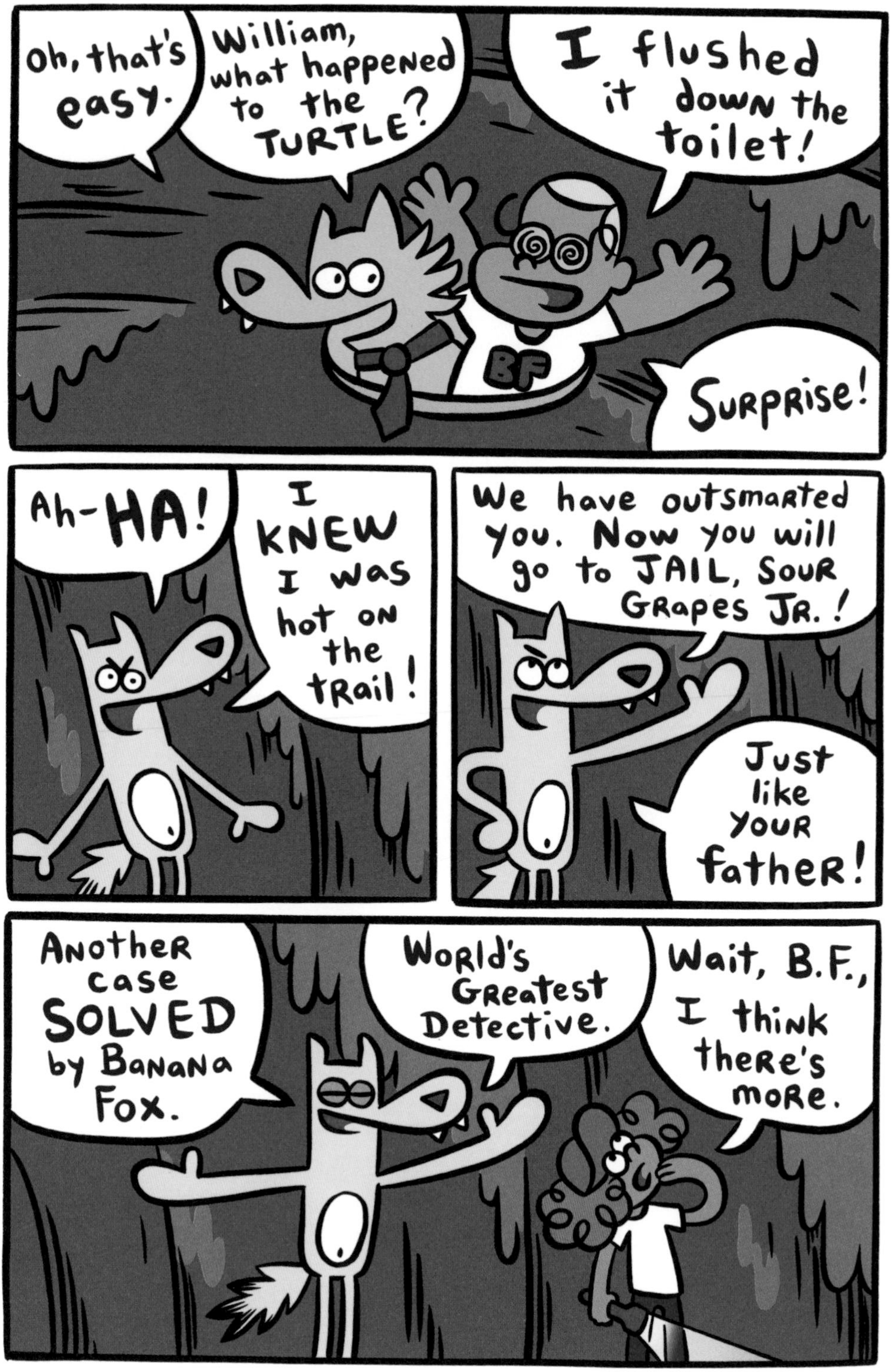
Oh, that's easy.
William, what happened to the TURTLE?
I flushed it down the toilet!
Surprise!
Ah-HA!
I KNEW I was hot on the trail!
We have outsmarted you. Now you will go to JAIL, SOUR GRAPES JR.!
Just like YOUR father!
Another case SOLVED by Banana Fox.
World's Greatest Detective.
Wait, B.F., I think there's more.

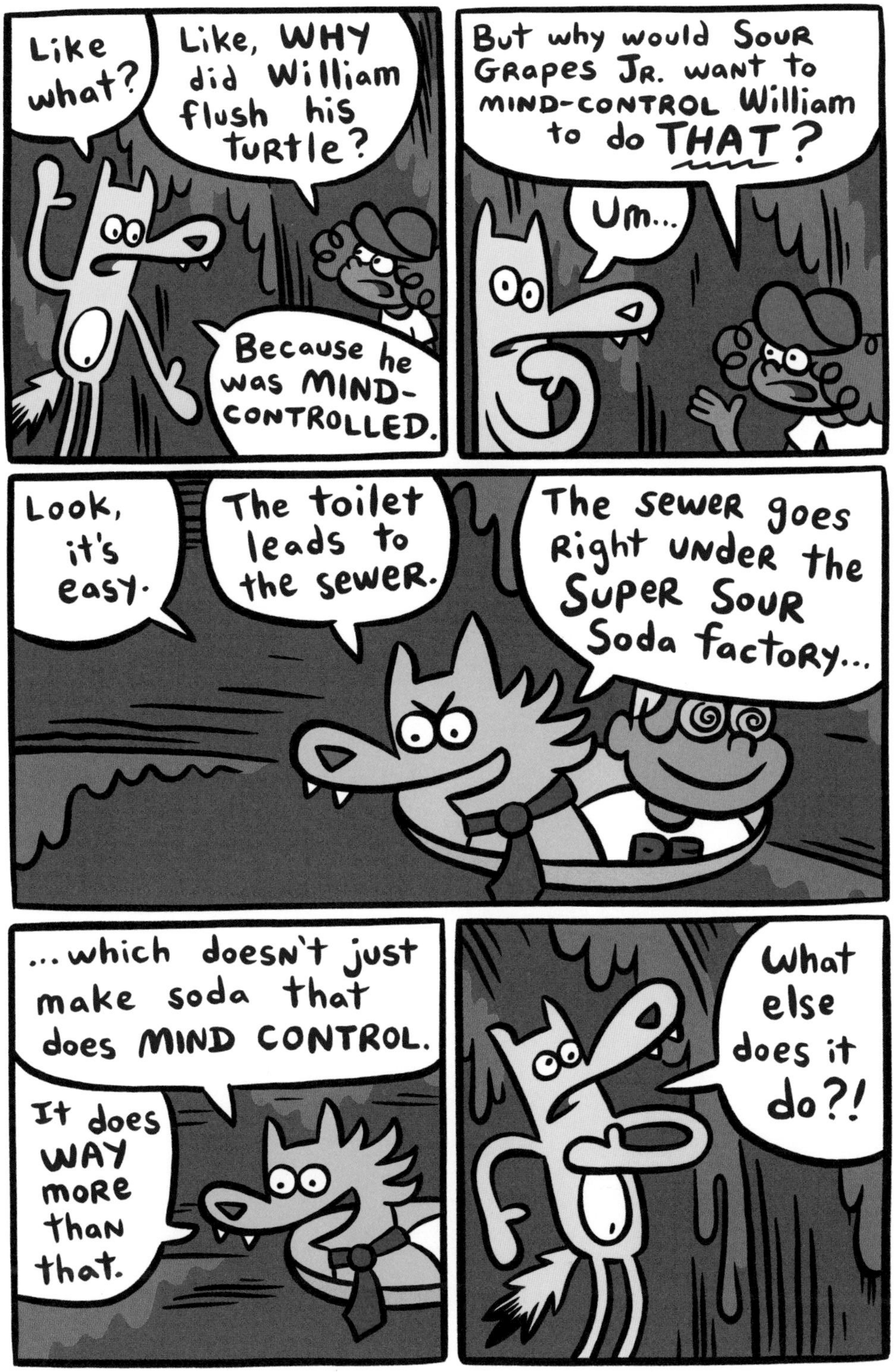
Like what?
Like, WHY did William flush his turtle?
Because he was MIND-CONTROLLED.
But why would SOUR GRAPES JR. want to MIND-CONTROL William to do THAT?
Um...
Look, it's easy.
The toilet leads to the sewer.
The sewer goes right under the SUPER SOUR Soda factory...
...which doesn't just make soda that does MIND CONTROL.
It does WAY more than that.
What else does it do?!

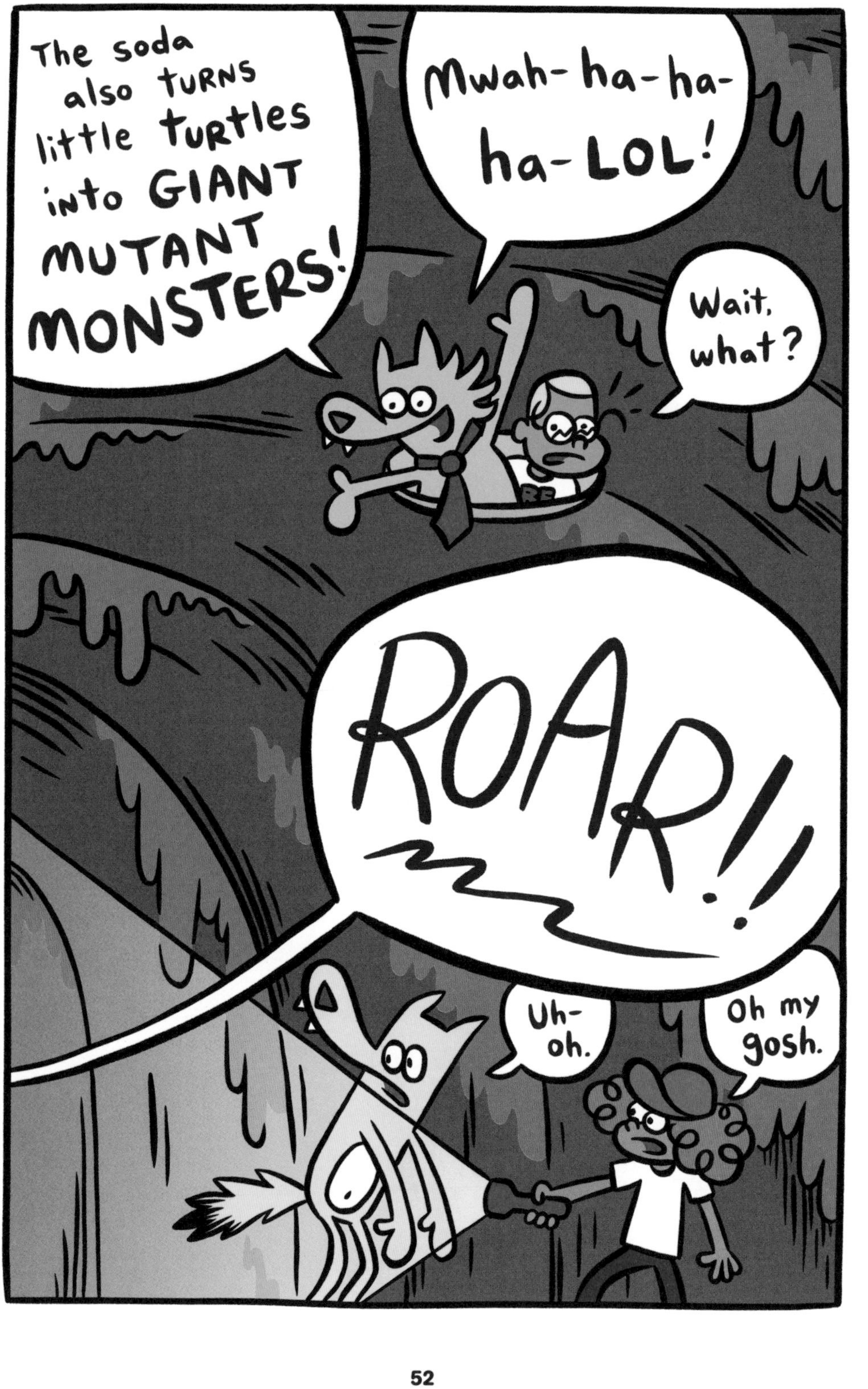
The soda also TURNS little turtles into GIANT MUTANT MONSTERS!
Mwah-ha-ha-ha-LOL!
Wait, what?
ROAR!!
Uh-oh.
Oh my gosh.

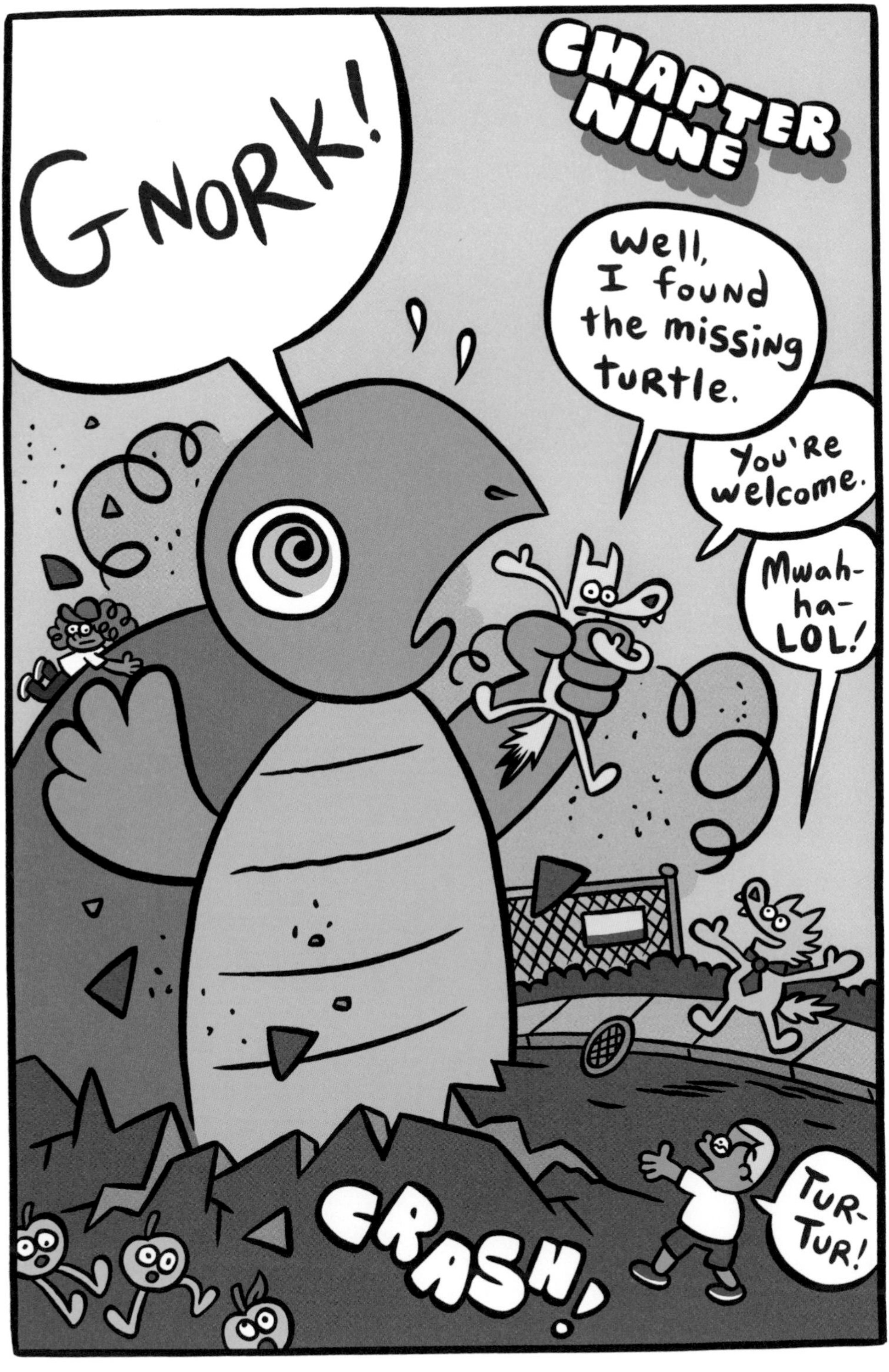
CHAPTER NINE
GNORK!
Well, I found the missing turtle.
You're welcome.
Mwah-ha-LOL!
CRASH!
TUR-TUR!

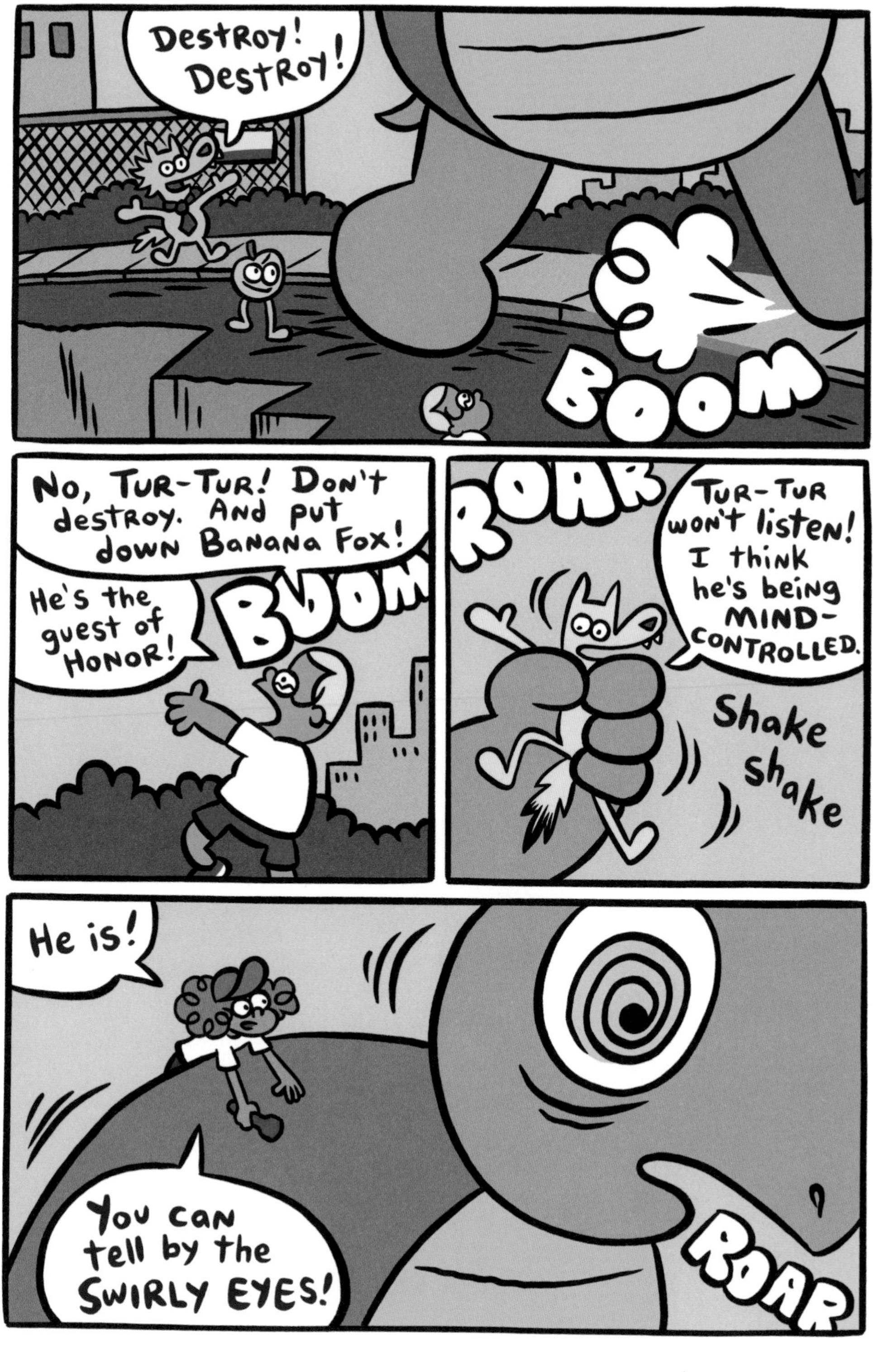

Destroy! Destroy!
BOOM
No, TUR-TUR! Don't destroy. And put down Banana Fox!
He's the guest of HONOR!
BOOM
ROAR
TUR-TUR won't listen! I think he's being MIND-CONTROLLED.
Shake shake
He is!
You can tell by the SWIRLY EYES!
ROAR

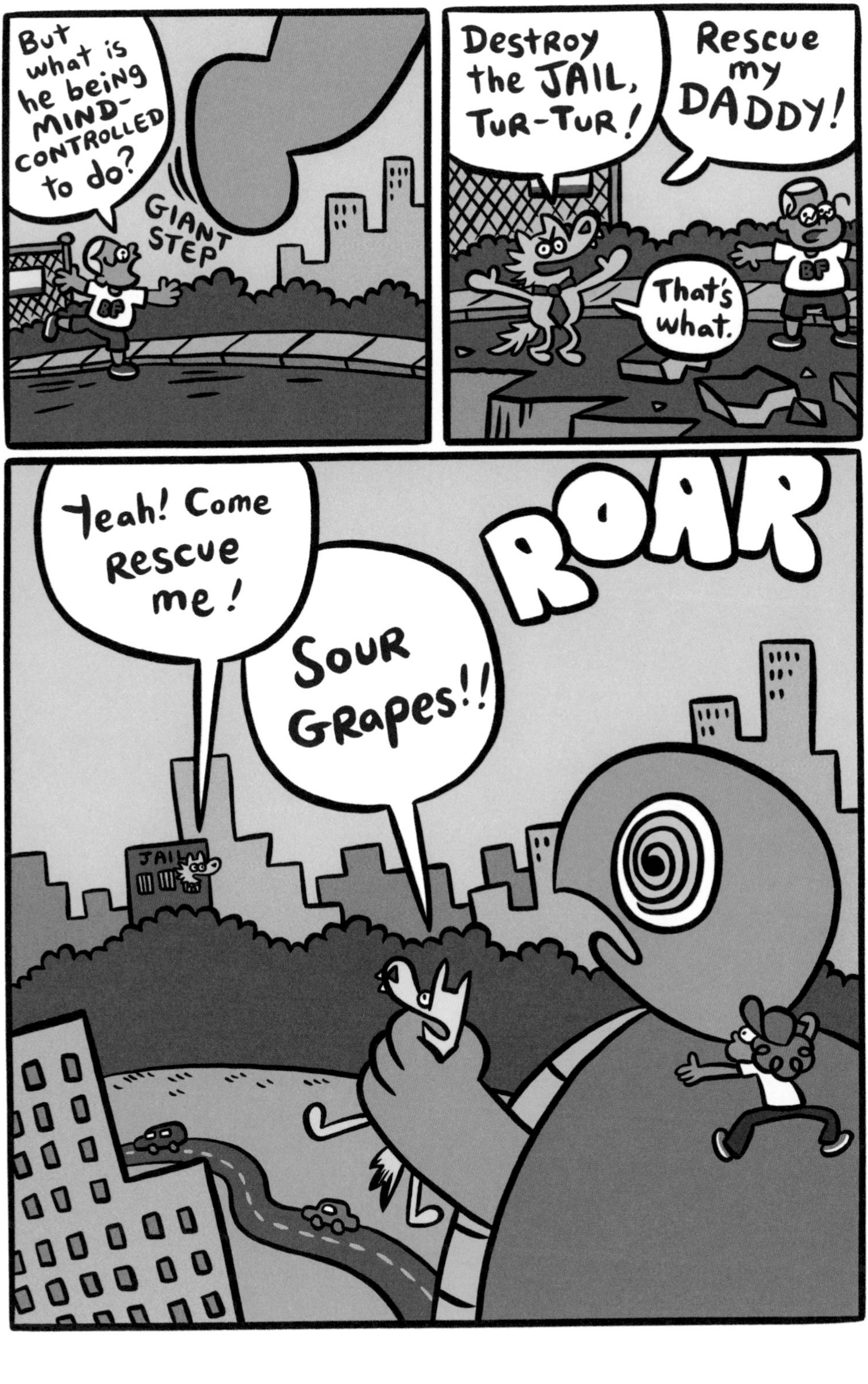
But what is he being MIND-CONTROLLED to do?
GIANT STEP
Destroy the JAIL, TUR-TUR!
Rescue my DADDY!
That's what.
Yeah! Come rescue me!
SOUR GRAPES!!
ROAR
JAIL

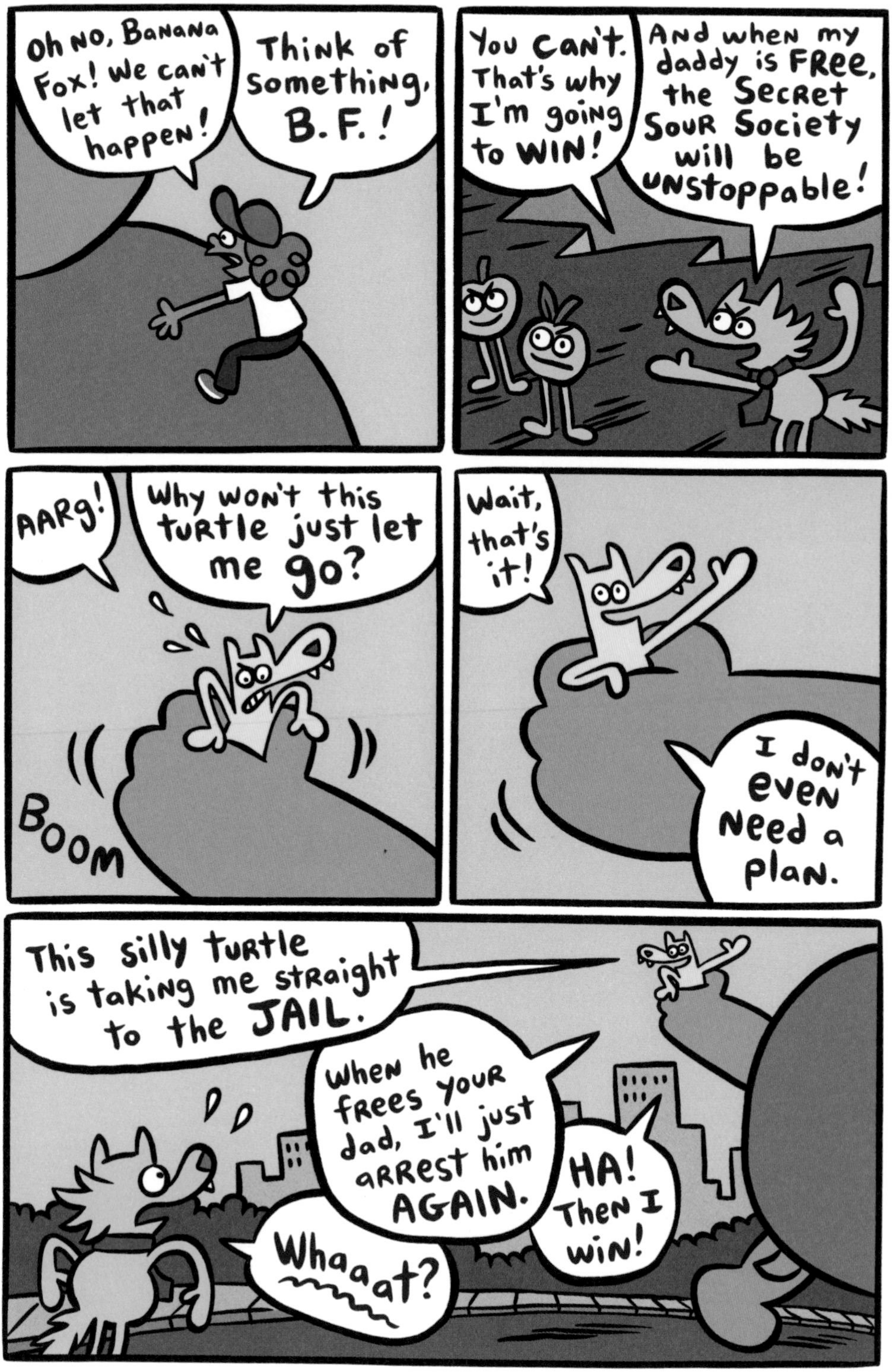

Oh NO, Banana Fox! We can't let that happen!
Think of something, B.F.!
You can't. That's why I'm going to WIN!
And when my daddy is FREE, the Secret Sour Society will be UNSTOPPABLE!
AARG!
Why won't this turtle just let me go?
BOOM
Wait, that's it!
I don't even need a plan.
This silly turtle is taking me straight to the JAIL.
When he frees your dad, I'll just arrest him AGAIN.
HA! Then I win!
Whaaaat?

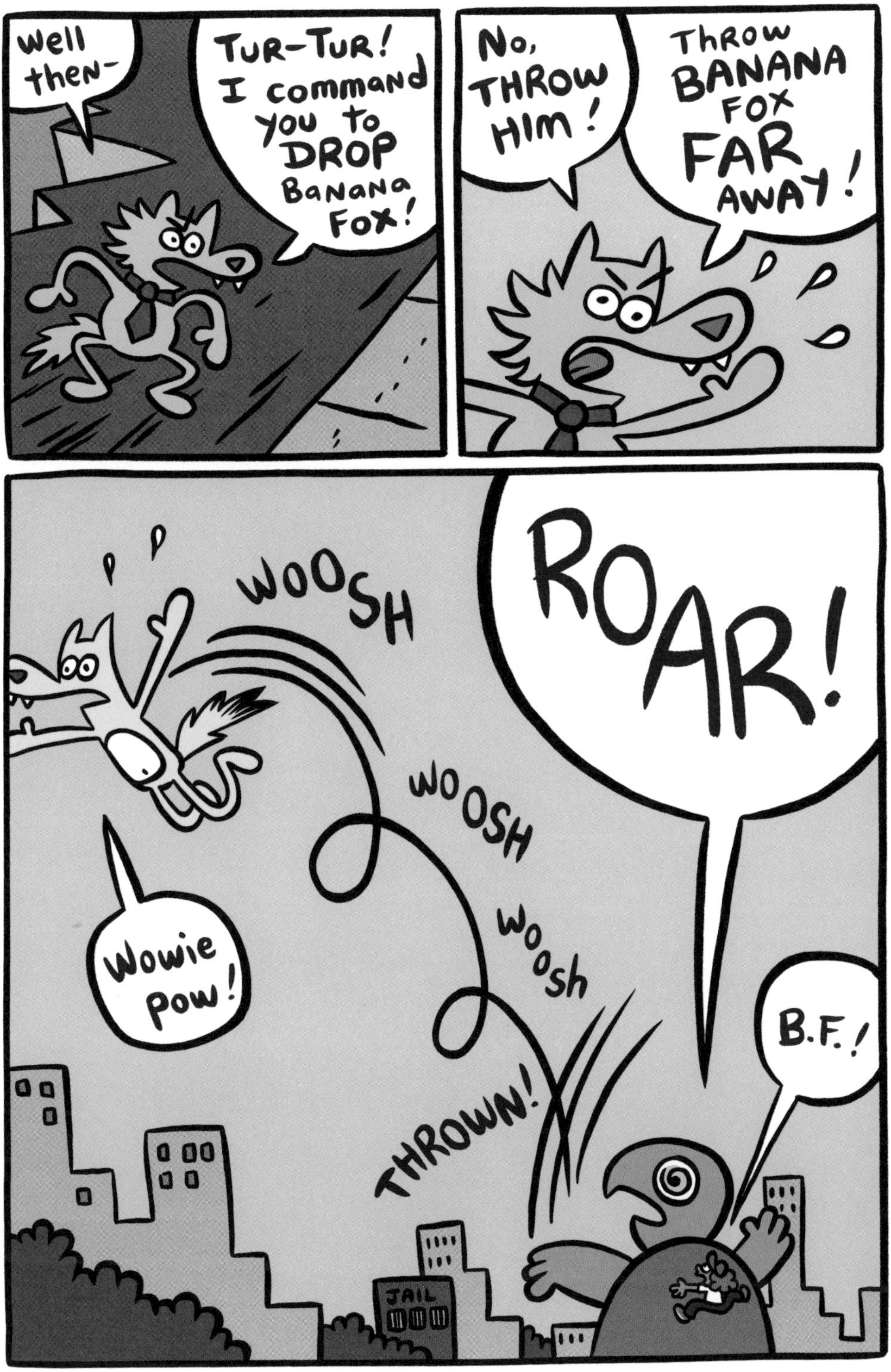
Well then-
TUR-TUR! I command you to DROP Banana Fox!
No, THROW HIM!
Throw BANANA FOX FAR AWAY!
ROAR!
WOOSH
WOOSH
WOOSH
Wowie pow!
B.F.!
THROWN!
JAIL

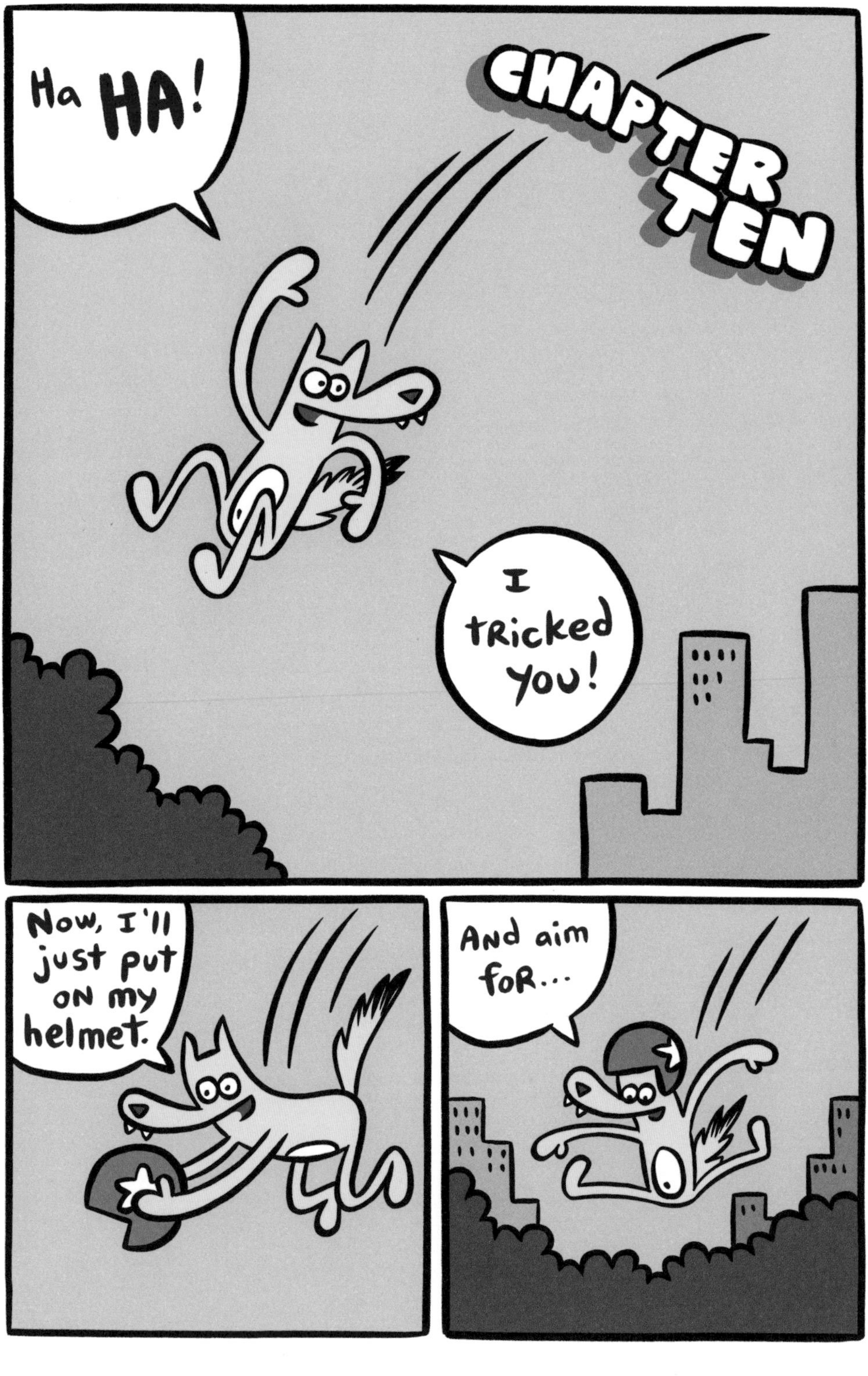
Ha HA!
CHAPTER TEN
I tricked you!
Now, I'll just put on my helmet.
And aim for...

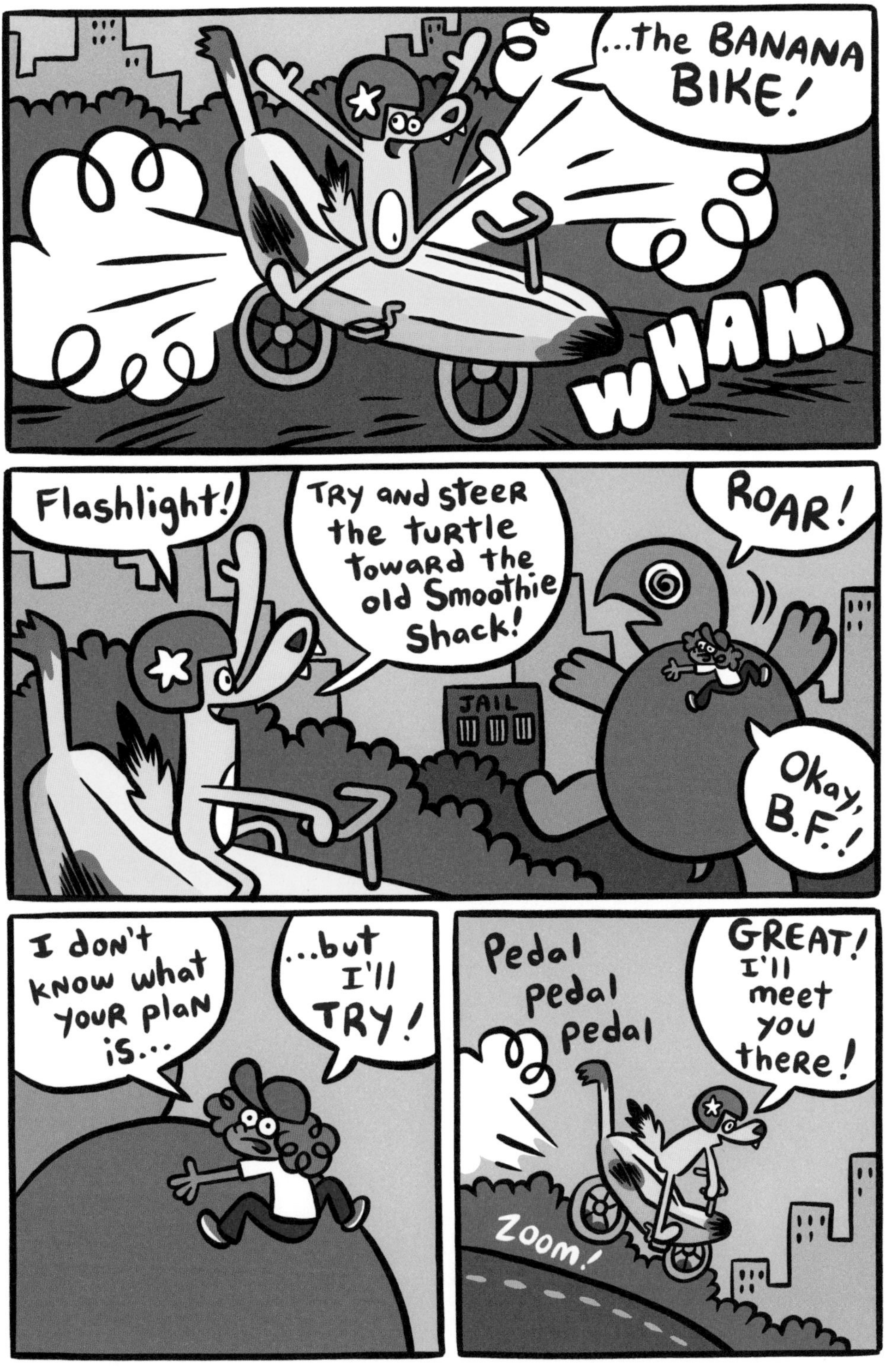
...the BANANA BIKE!
WHAM
Flashlight!
TRY and STEER the turtle toward the old Smoothie Shack!
ROAR!
JAIL
Okay, B.F.!
I don't know what your plan is...
...but I'll TRY!
Pedal pedal pedal
GREAT! I'll meet you there!
ZOOM!

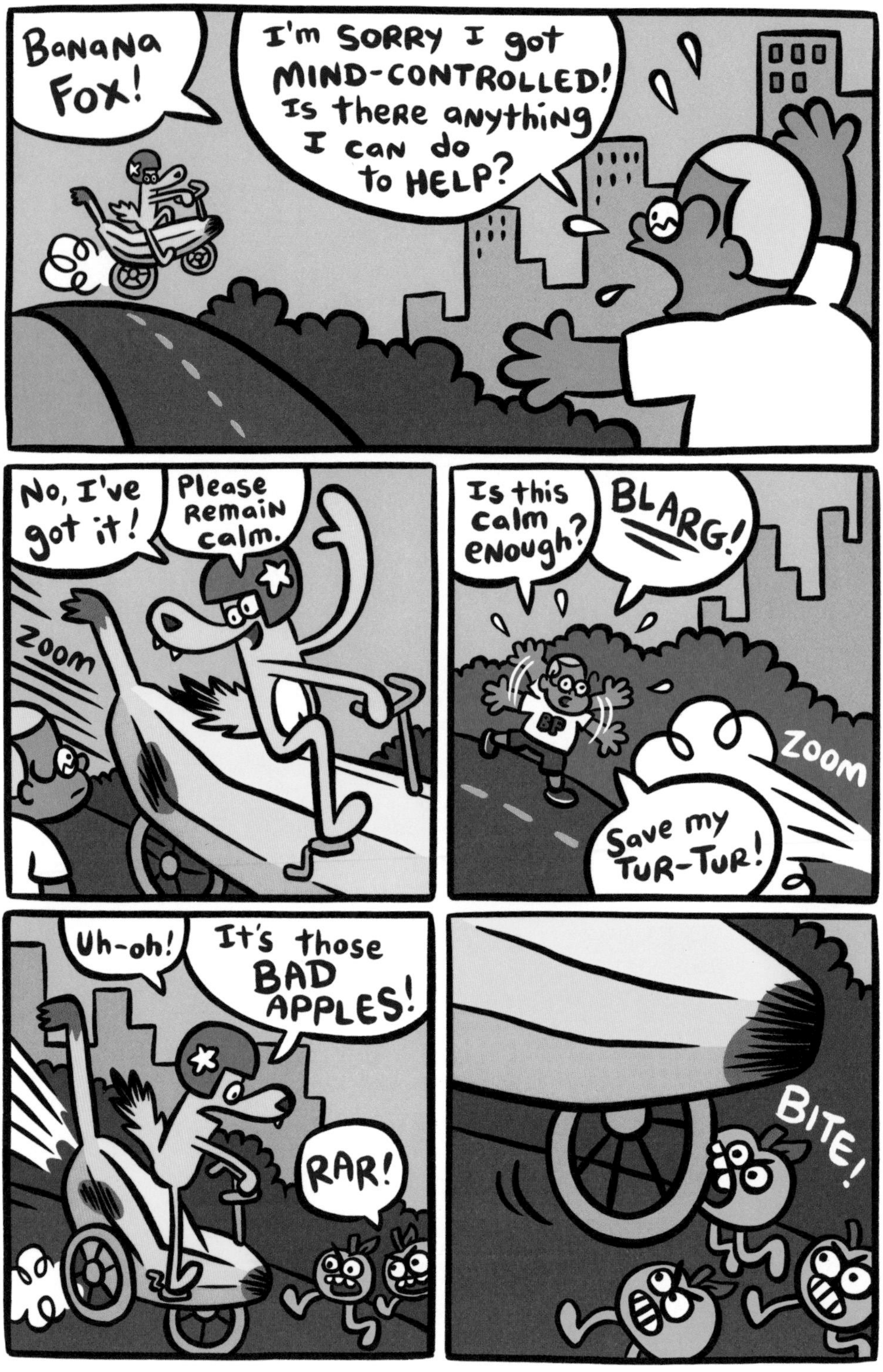

Banana Fox!
I'm SORRY I got MIND-CONTROLLED! Is there anything I can do to HELP?
No, I've got it!
Please remain calm.
ZOOM
Is this calm enough?
BLARG!
BF
ZOOM
Save my TUR-TUR!
Uh-oh!
It's those BAD APPLES!
RAR!
BITE!

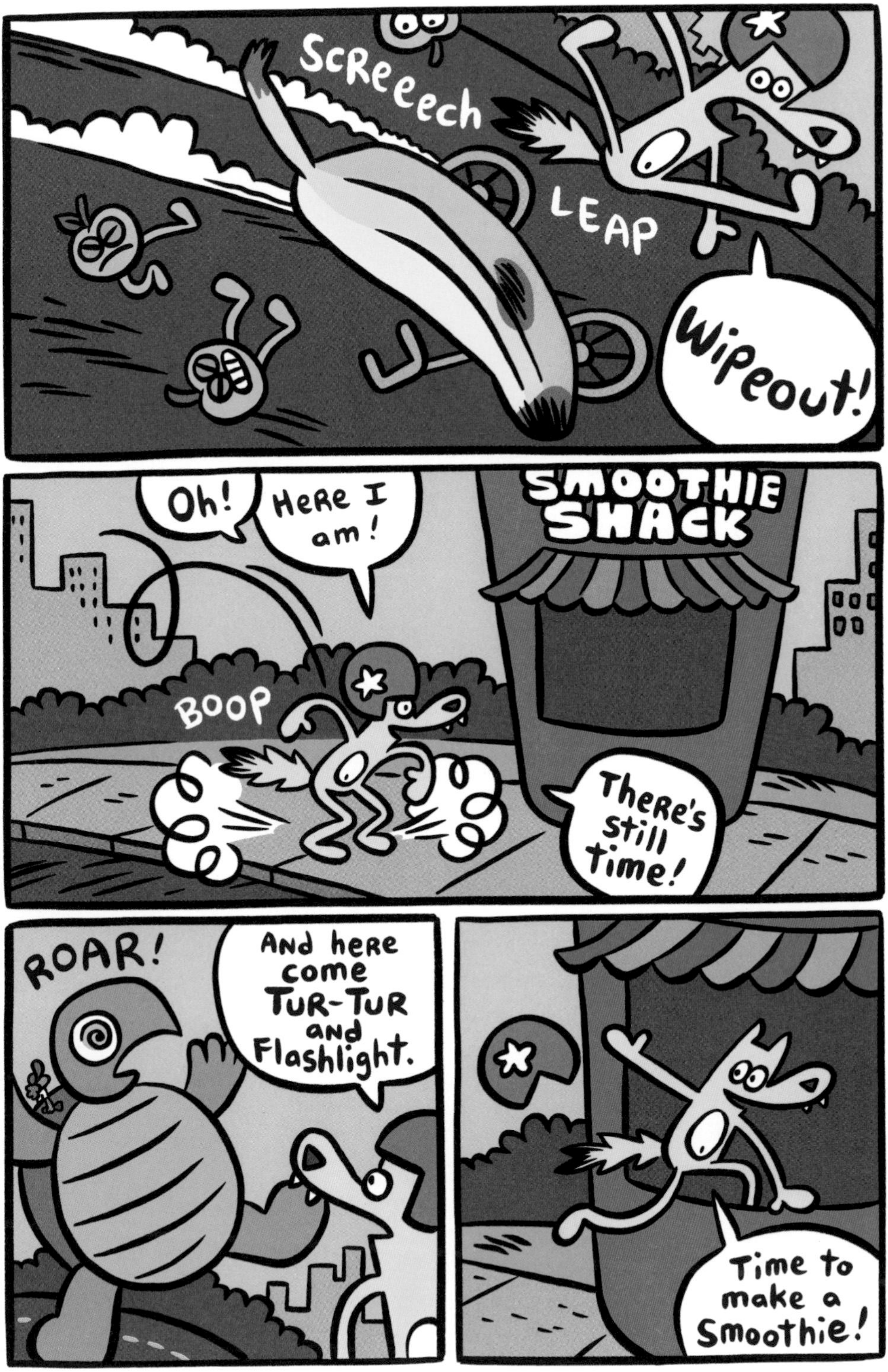
SCREEECH
LEAP
Wipeout!
Oh!
Here I am!
SMOOTHIE SHACK
BOOP
There's still time!
ROAR!
And here come TUR-TUR and Flashlight.
Time to make a Smoothie!

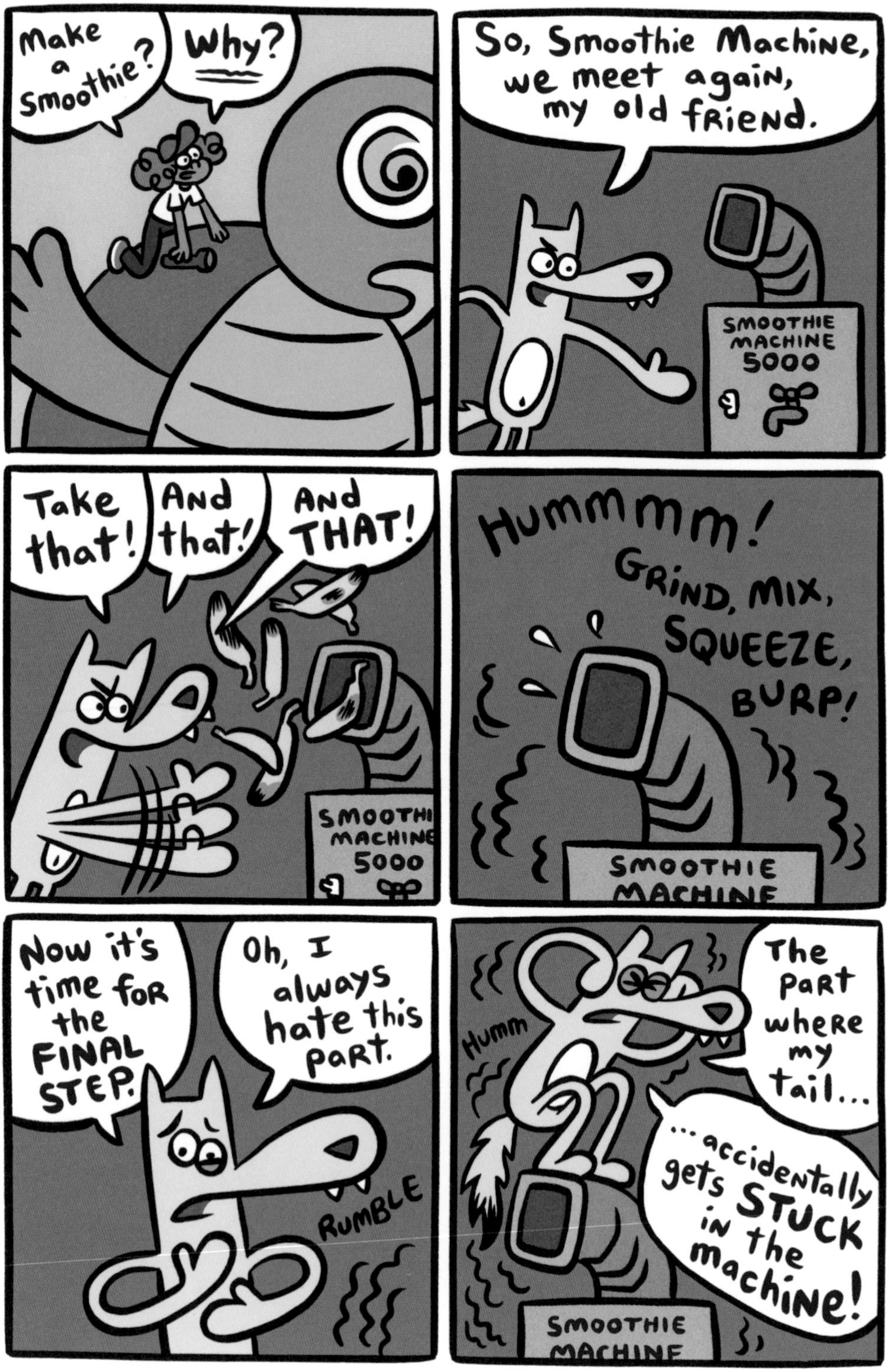
Make a smoothie?
Why?
So, Smoothie Machine, we meet again, my old friend.
SMOOTHIE MACHINE 5000
Take that!
And that!
And THAT!
SMOOTHIE MACHINE 5000
Hummmmm!
GRIND, MIX, SQUEEZE, BURP!
SMOOTHIE
Now it's time for the FINAL STEP.
Oh, I always hate this part.
RUMBLE
Humm
The part where my tail...
...accidentally gets STUCK in the machine!
SMOOTHIE

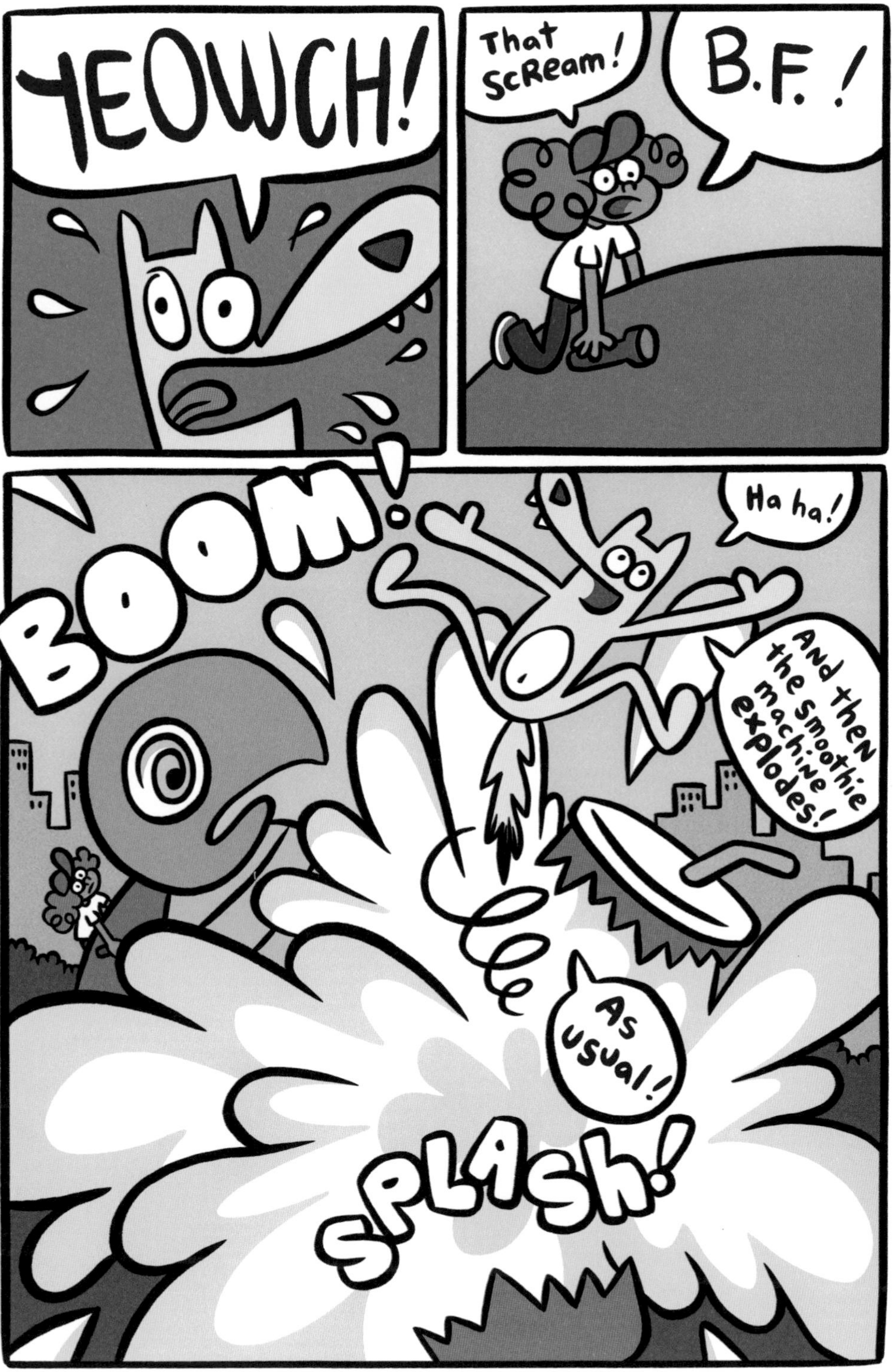
YEOWCH!
That scream!
B.F.!
BOOM!
Ha ha!
And then the smoothie machine explodes!
As usual!
SPLASH!

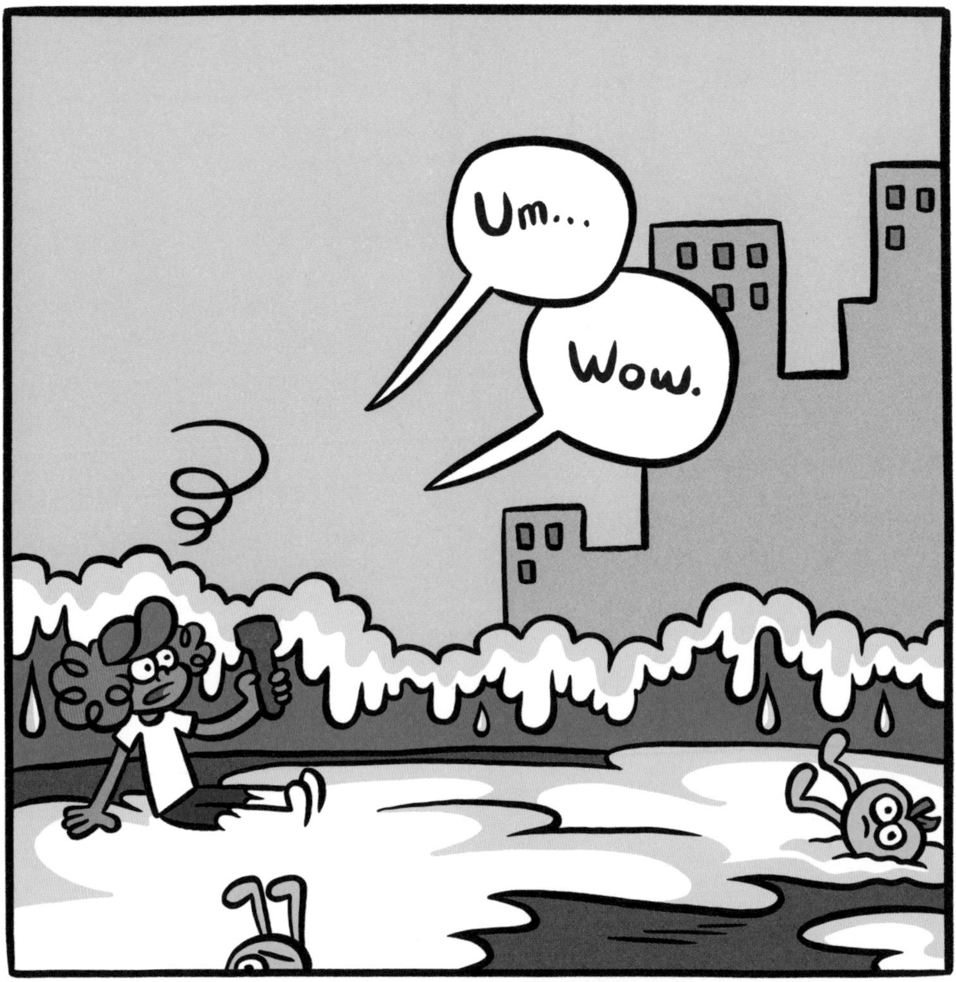
Um...
Wow.

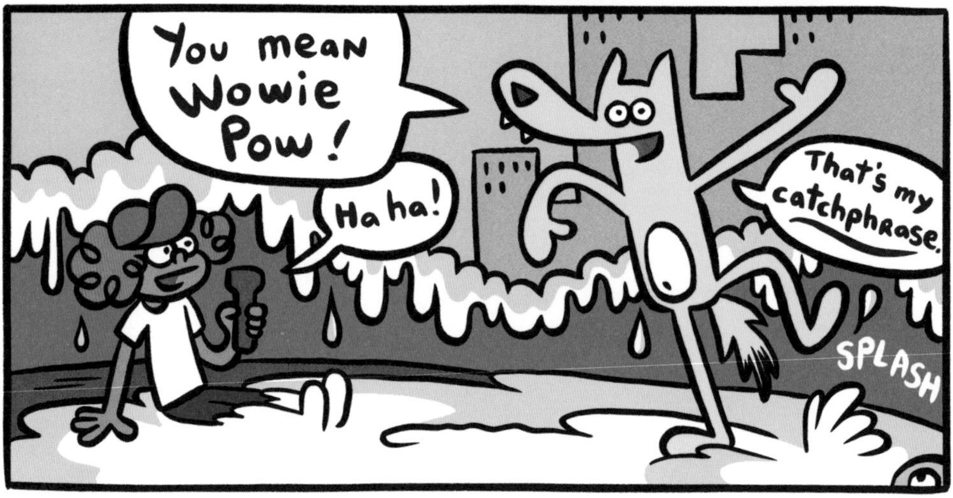
You mean Wowie Pow!
Ha ha!
That's my catchphrase.
SPLASH

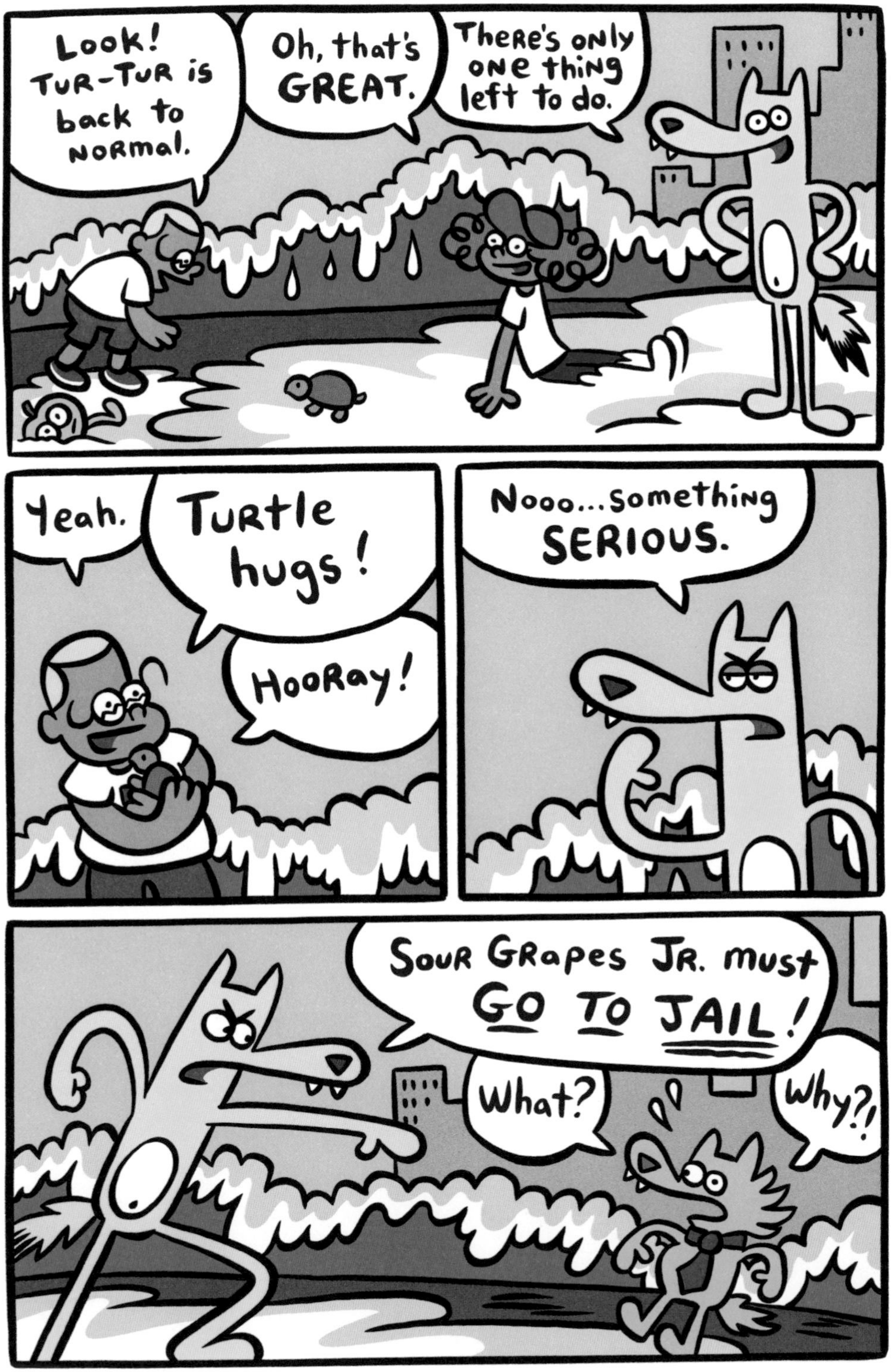
Look! TUR-TUR is back to NORMAL.
Oh, that's GREAT.
There's only one thing left to do.
Yeah.
Turtle hugs!
HooRay!
Nooo...something SERIOUS.
Sour Grapes Jr. must GO TO JAIL!
What?
Why?!

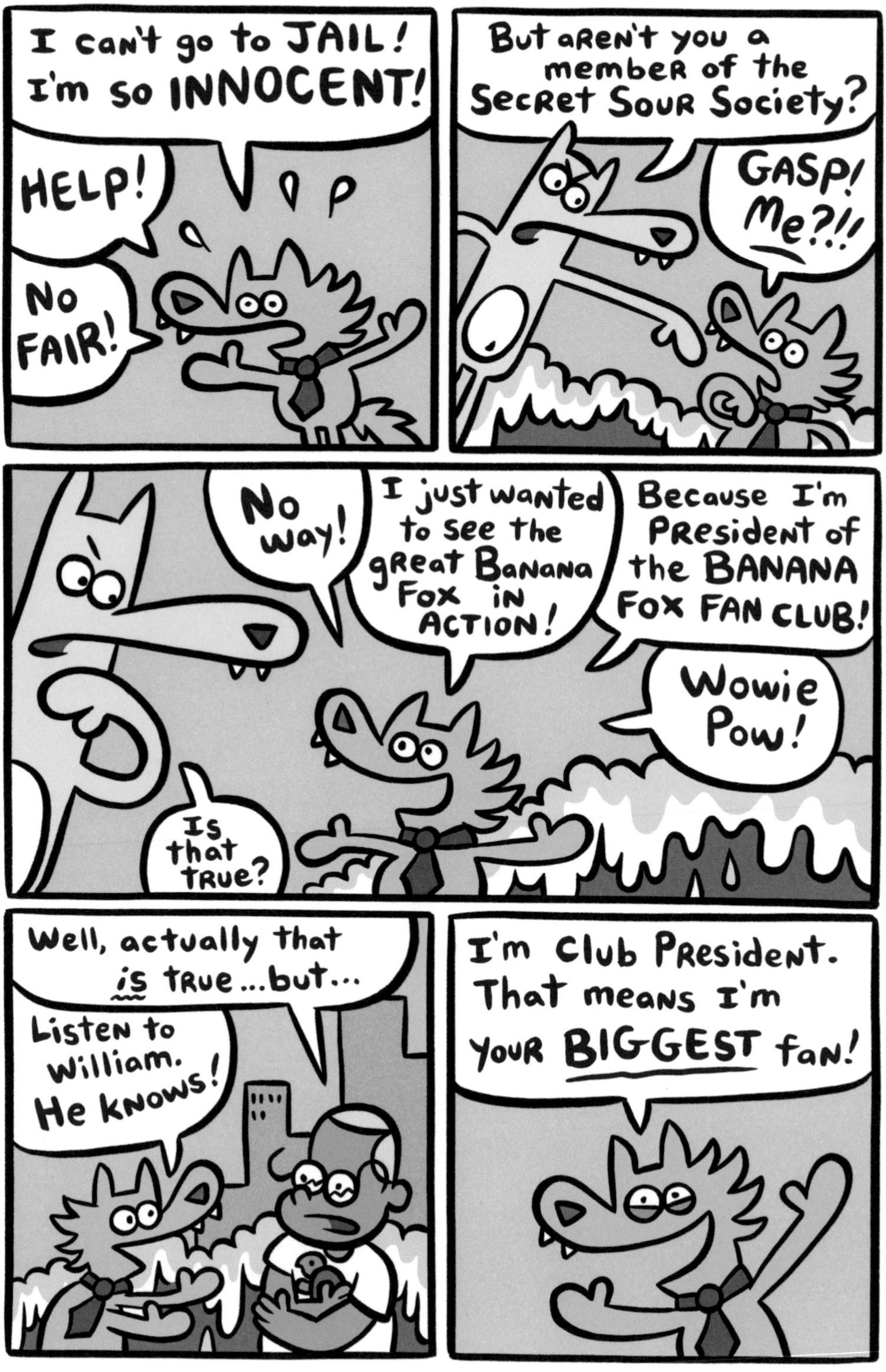
I can't go to JAIL! I'm so INNOCENT!
HELP!
NO FAIR!
But aren't you a member of the Secret Sour Society?
GASP! Me?!!
No way!
I just wanted to see the great Banana Fox in ACTION!
Because I'm President of the BANANA FOX FAN CLUB!
Wowie Pow!
Is that true?
Well, actually that is true...but...
Listen to William. He knows!
I'm Club President. That means I'm your BIGGEST fan!

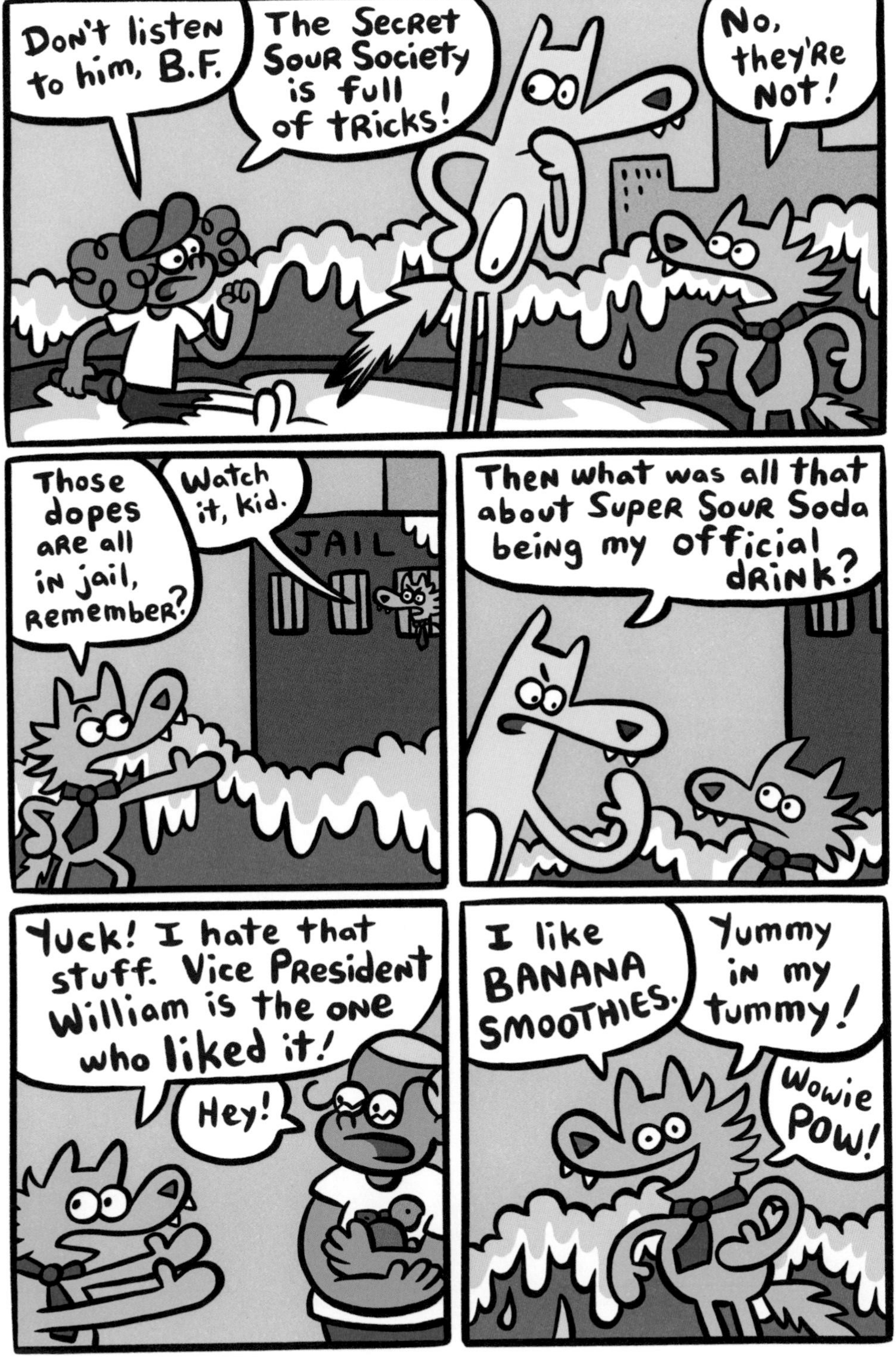
Don't listen to him, B.F.
The Secret Sour Society is full of tricks!
No, they're NOT!
Those dopes are all in jail, remember?
Watch it, kid.
JAIL
Then what was all that about Super Sour Soda being my official drink?
Yuck! I hate that stuff. Vice President William is the one who liked it!
Hey!
I like BANANA SMOOTHIES.
Yummy in my tummy!
Wowie POW!

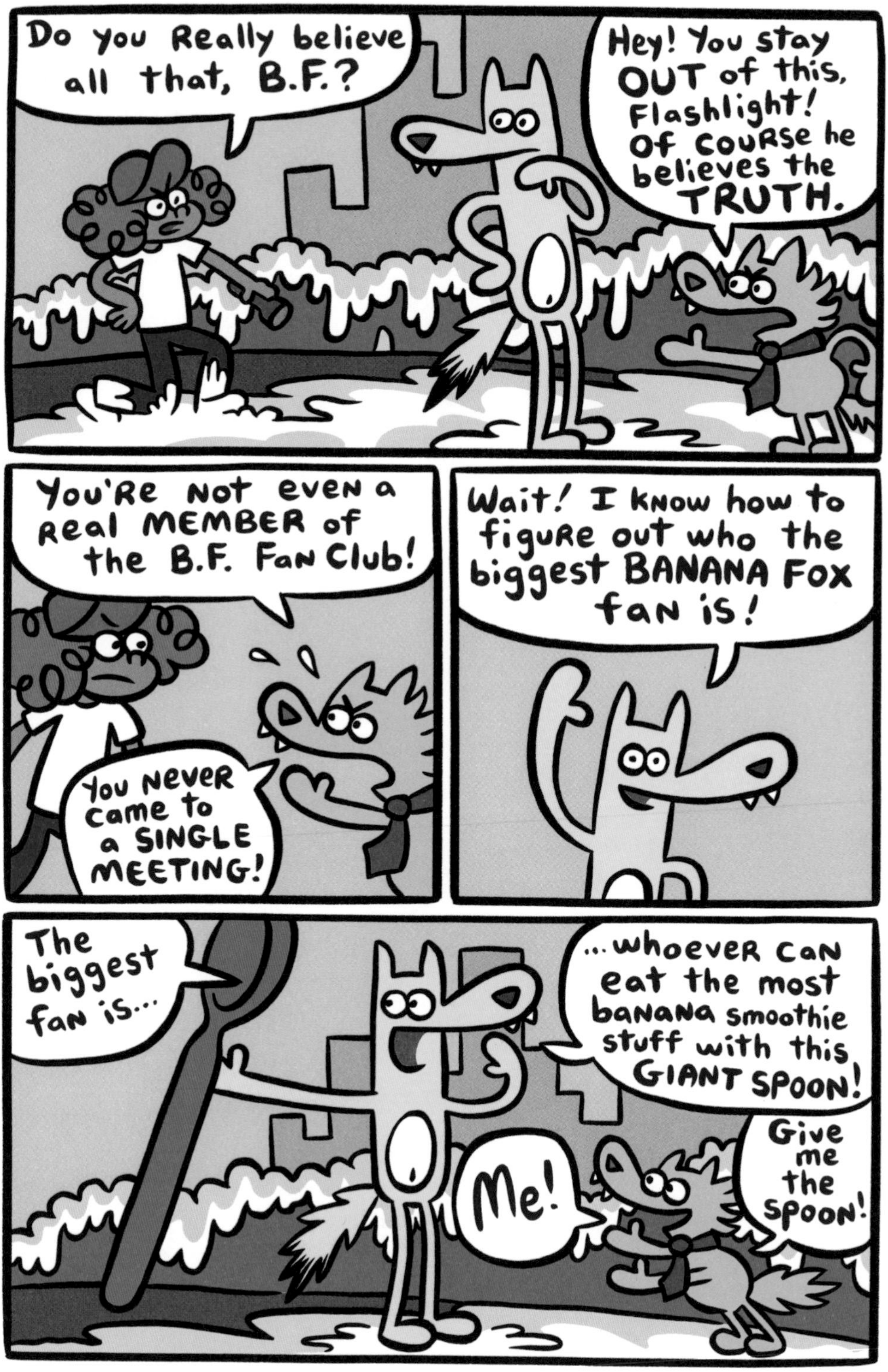
Do you Really believe all that, B.F.?
Hey! You stay OUT of this, Flashlight! Of course he believes the TRUTH.
You're not even a real MEMBER of the B.F. Fan Club!
You never came to a SINGLE MEETING!
Wait! I know how to figure out who the biggest BANANA FOX fan is!
The biggest fan is...
...whoever can eat the most banana smoothie stuff with this GIANT SPOON!
Me!
Give me the spoon!

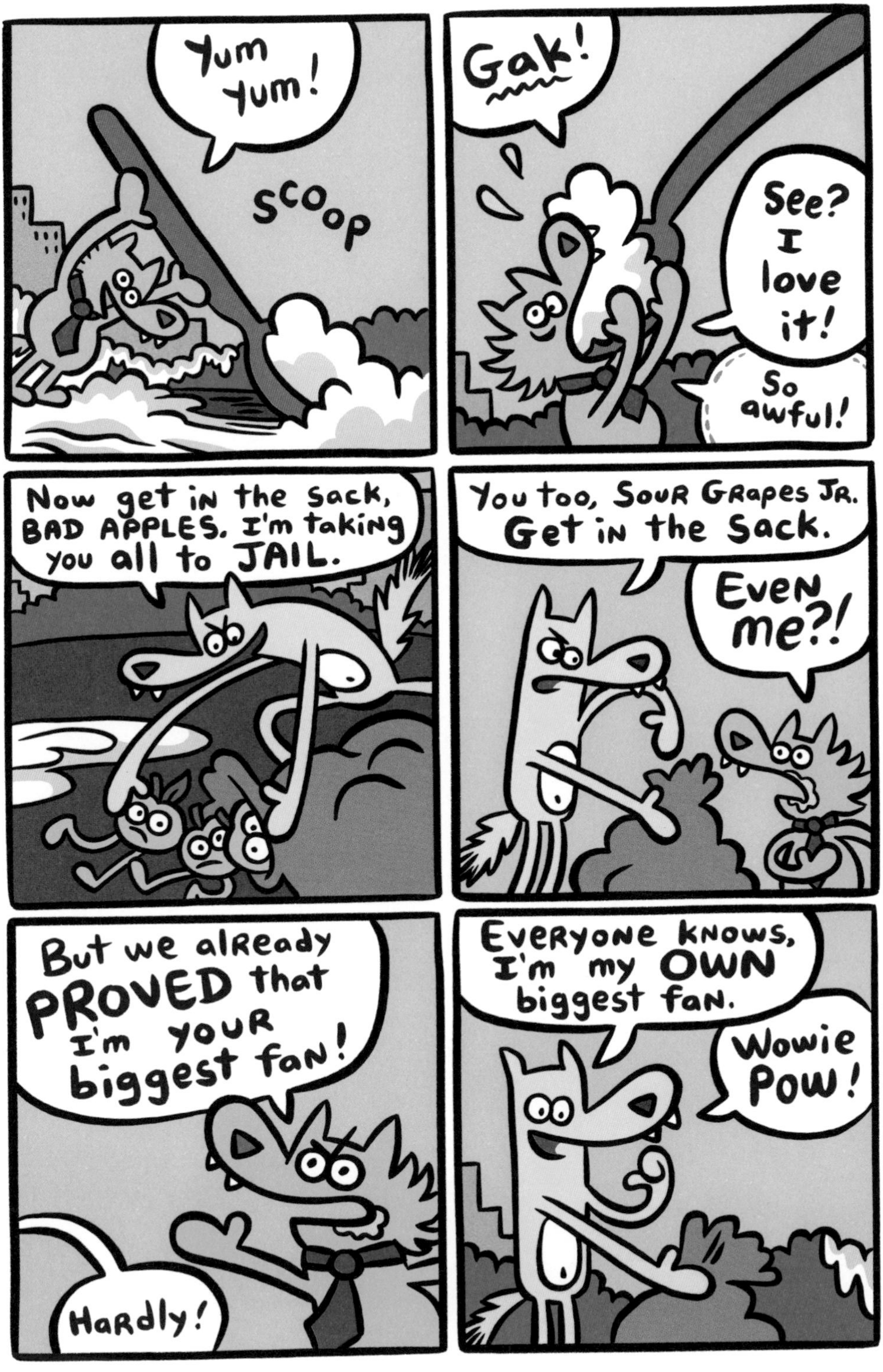
Yum yum!
SCOOP
Gak!
See? I love it!
So awful!
Now get in the sack, BAD APPLES. I'm taking you all to JAIL.
You too, SOUR GRAPES JR. Get in the sack.
Even me?!
But we already PROVED that I'm YOUR biggest fan!
Hardly!
Everyone knows, I'm my OWN biggest fan.
Wowie Pow!

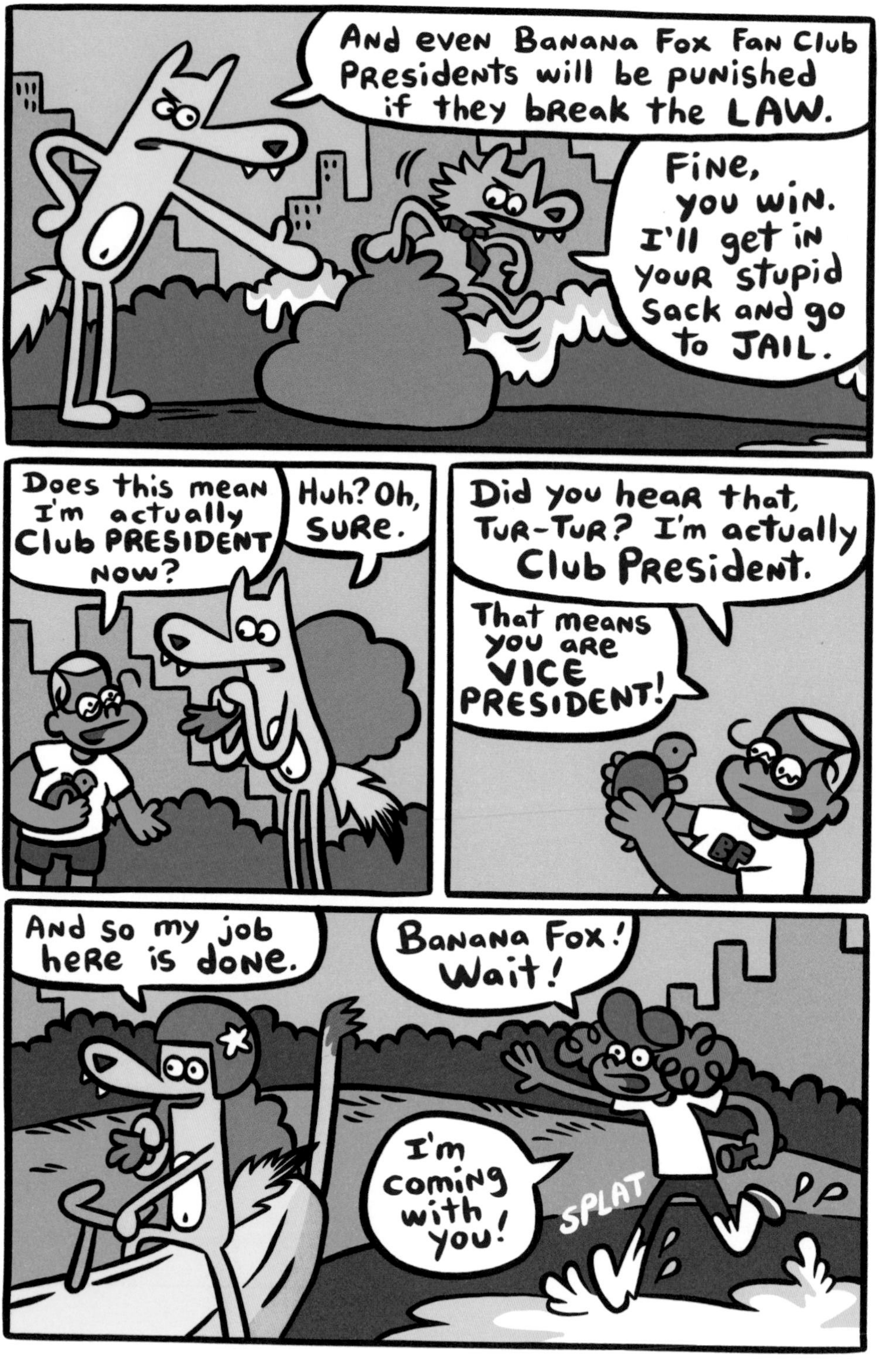
And even Banana Fox Fan Club Presidents will be punished if they break the LAW.
Fine, you win. I'll get in your stupid Sack and go to JAIL.
Does this mean I'm actually Club PRESIDENT now?
Huh? Oh, SURE.
Did you hear that, TUR-TUR? I'm actually Club President.
That means you are VICE PRESIDENT!
BF
And so my job here is done.
Banana Fox! Wait!
I'm coming with you!
SPLAT

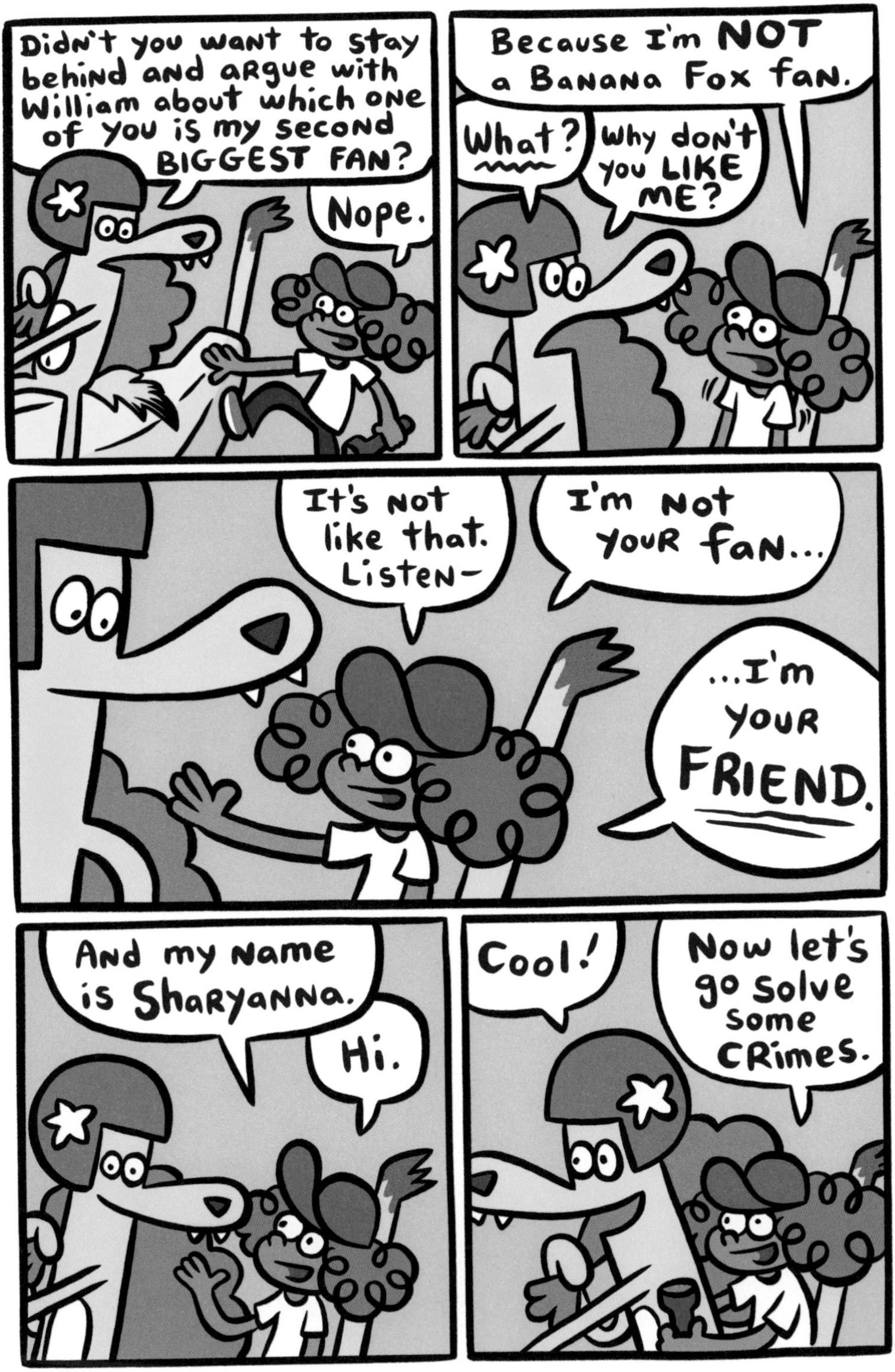
Didn't you want to stay behind and argue with William about which one of you is my second BIGGEST FAN?
Nope.
Because I'm NOT a Banana Fox fan.
What?
Why don't you LIKE ME?
It's not like that. Listen—
I'm not your fan...
...I'm your FRIEND.
And my name is Sharyanna.
Hi.
Cool!
Now let's go solve some crimes.

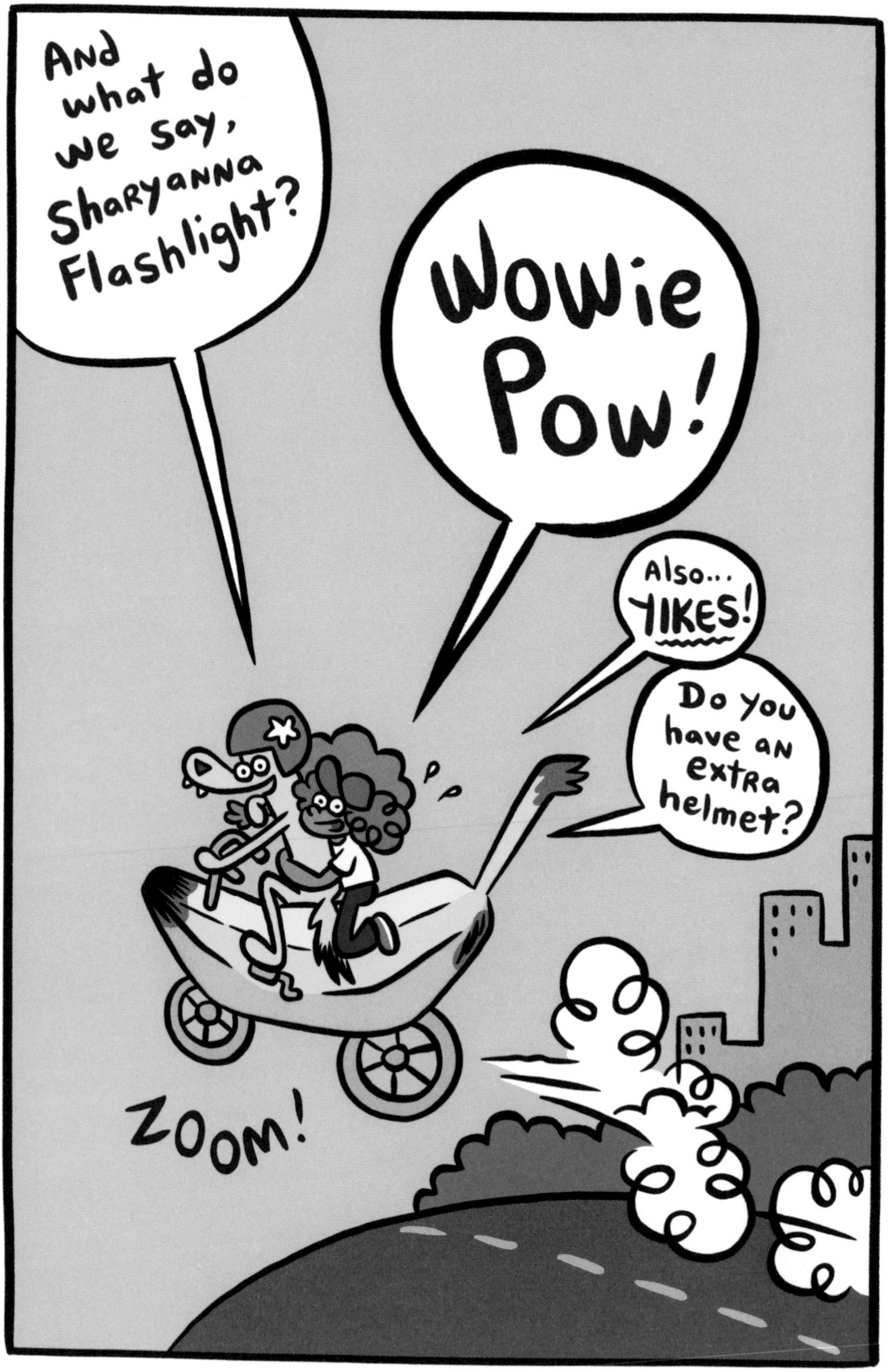
And what do we say, Sharyanna Flashlight?
Wowie Pow!
Also... YIKES!
Do you have an extra helmet?
ZOOM!

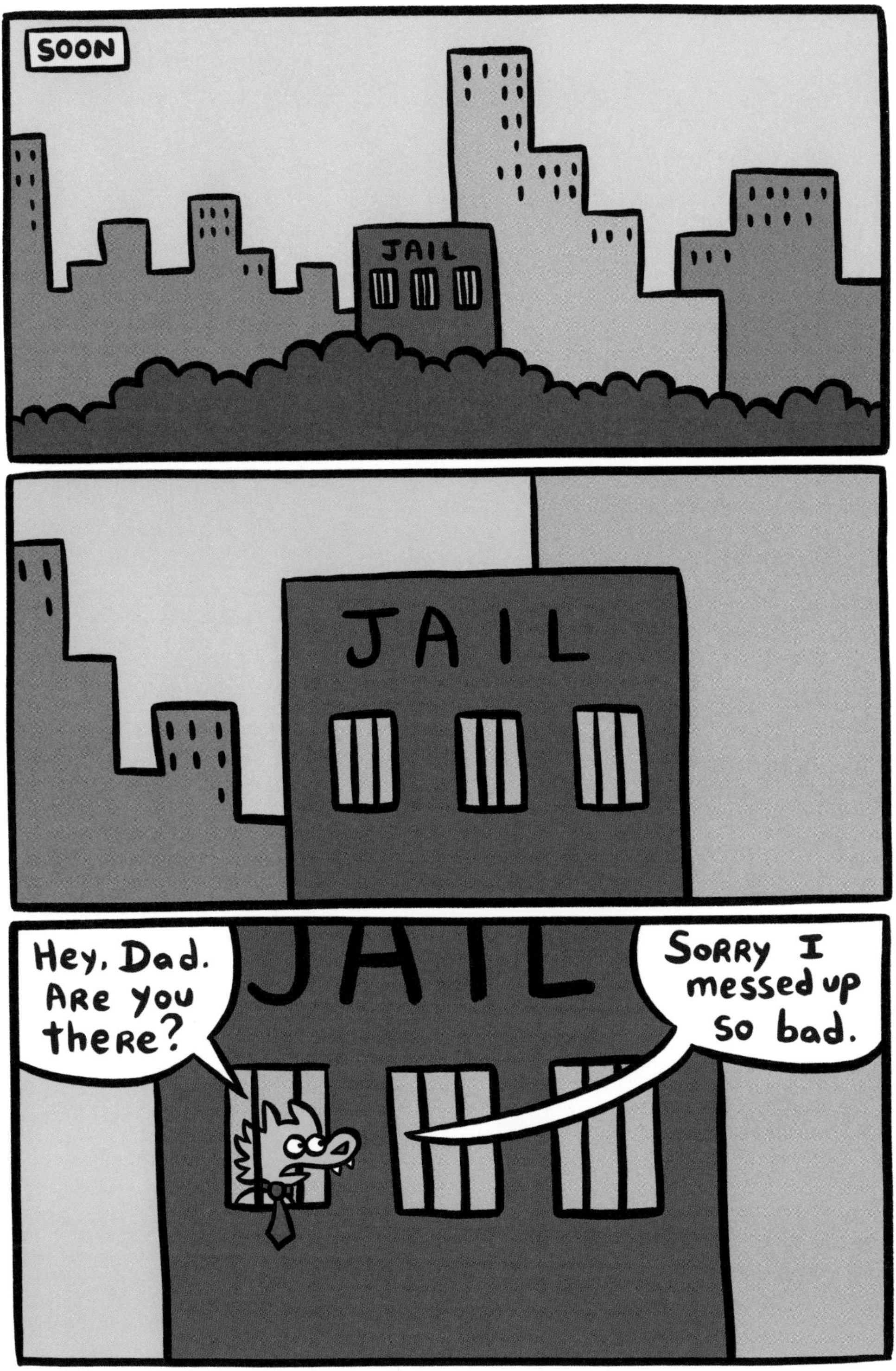

SOON
JAIL
JAIL
JAIL
Hey, Dad. Are you there?
Sorry I messed up so bad.

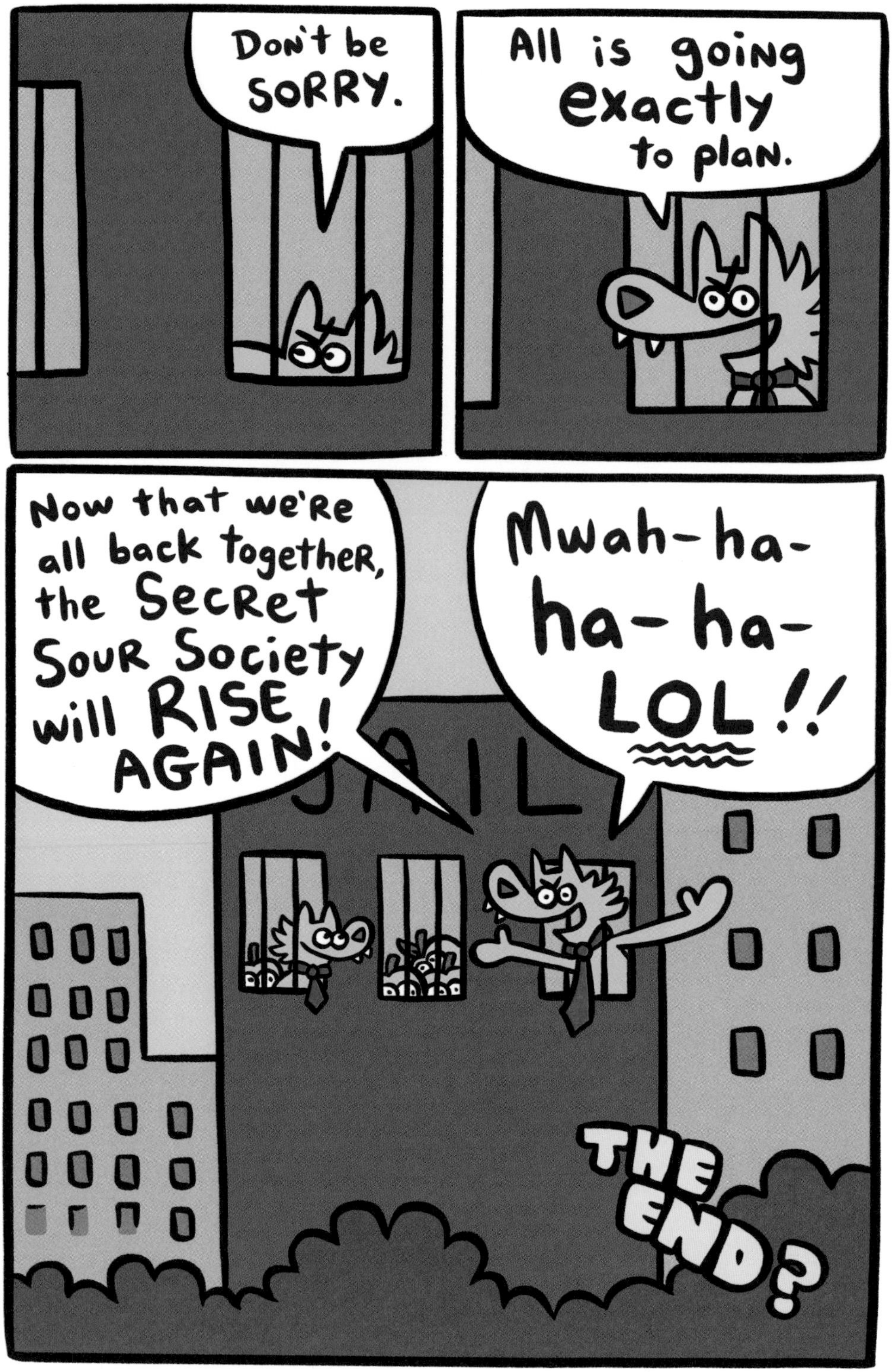
Don't be SORRY.
All is going exactly to plan.
Now that we're all back together, the Secret Sour Society will RISE AGAIN!
Mwah-ha-ha-ha-LOL!!
JAIL
THE END?

JAMES KOCHALKA

is one of the most unique and prolific cartoonists working in America today. His comics have been published internationally, and he's developed animated cartoons for Nickelodeon. Among his best known work is the Johnny Boo series, for which he won an Eisner Award in 2019. In 2011, James became the first official cartoonist laureate of the state of Vermont, where he lives with his wife, Amy; their two sons; and their cats.